BOOKARAZZI BLACKMAIL

A SHELF INDULGENCE COZY MYSTERY

S.E. BABIN

Bookarazzi Blackmail Copyright 2024 © S.E. Babin

Cover art by Lou Harper from Cover Affairs

Published by Oliver-Heber Books

0 9 8 7 6 5 4 3 2 1

ONE

The annual twenty-five percent off sale at Tattered Pages brought so many people into the store, it sent a line out the door and around the corner. Harper sagged against the counter once there was a lull in customers crowding around the register and from the line that had to be annoying the other store owners scattered around my shop. It was almost closing time.

"Ugh," she breathed. "This is a picture-perfect example of people coming out of the woodwork for a good deal."

I laughed. "It's a good way to get rid of old stock." It was true. If people thought it was on sale, they were a lot more willing to buy it. I'd discounted a lot of books I hadn't been able to move previously, and they were selling like hotcakes.

"I can't believe people are buying math books." Harper

shuddered. "Of all the things to go into a bookstore for, math is the least likely reason."

I had to agree. "Not everyone loves fiction as much as we do."

"Yeah, but *math*?" Harper's nose wrinkled.

"Few people can resist the allure of a good deal," I said. "Even if it's math."

The bell over the door rang, revealing Daniel Jensen carrying a large box. His face lit up when he saw me. "Hey!" He shook the box. "Look what I brought!"

I rushed over and held the door open for him. "If it's your new release, and it's early, I might have to kiss you," I breathed.

His eyes brightened. "Well, pucker up, Dakota, because it's both."

Harper snickered and headed to the back. For some reason, she always left me alone when Daniel entered the shop. She was a little matchmaker at heart.

But there was no matchmaking to be had here. Daniel and I were still firmly in the friend zone. He wanted to step over the line into something more, and I was the stalwart guard refusing to waver from my position.

The amazing thing about Daniel, though, was he never pushed for more. While he wasn't exactly content, I suspected Daniel was playing the long game.

The bell jingled again, revealing Hardy, the big reason Daniel was still in the friend zone.

Daniel, never missing an opportunity, grinned. "Gird

your loins, Detective. Dakota is about to lay a big ol' kiss on me."

I heard a bark of laughter come from the back.

"Oh?" Hardy's eyebrows lifted. "Care to share with the class?" His voice was mild, but I knew him well enough not to miss that flash of jealousy in his eyes.

"I brought her much anticipated gifts that no one else in the entire world has." Daniel winked at me. "Dakota is beyond excited and has decided to share that joy by granting me a kiss."

"Like a princess in a glass coffin in the woods," Hardy said mildly. "I wonder if you'll disappear once it's over."

Daniel laughed. I rolled my eyes. "Quit it, you two."

The two had formed an odd yet slightly antagonistic friendship. Frenemies, I guess I could call it. They liked and respected each other, but both were tussling for a prize I wasn't ready to grant.

Me.

Hardy and I dated for a while until his normal life collapsed around him in the form of an ex-fiancée and a beautiful little girl he later found out was his daughter. I was happy for him and only wanted the best for him, but I always imagined my life going a little differently.

I'd let him go to give him the time and focus he needed to figure out how to become a father, and he'd ended up with full-time custody and a warmer, softer disposition toward life.

My heart had broken, but it ended up being the best choice for everyone. Fatherhood agreed with him, and I liked this new version of Hardy even better than the old one.

Hardy made it no secret he wanted to get back together, but I wasn't ready for his new life, nor ready for the potential of being a stepmom. I was getting wildly ahead of myself, but Hardy and I had ended up very serious, very soon, and I knew the potential was there.

This tentative friendship we had with the three of us probably wouldn't last, but I would enjoy it while it did.

I made a gimme gesture for the box. Daniel grinned and slid it over the desk. Within seconds, I had it open and was pawing through the paper to get to the goodies.

A soft sound of excitement escaped me when I pulled out Daniel's newest release.

A Time for Murder. I grinned at him.

He shrugged. "We don't always get to pick our titles. I fought against this one, actually, but they insisted, and I need to pay my light bill."

"It won't matter," I said encouragingly. "Your readers will come regardless of the title."

"One would hope." Daniel shook his head. "I've been doing this for years, and every release, I think to myself, this is it. This is the one where they all abandon me, and I'll end up a miser in a dark room drinking whiskey and lamenting my glory days."

"Drama queen." I rolled my eyes but hugged the box. "Thanks for these. I promise I won't put them out until I'm allowed. But hopefully, it's soon?" I batted my eyelashes at him. "Pretty please."

"I don't make the schedule either." He waved his fingers at me. "All my magic comes from these and my brain. The rest of it comes from a highly organized team who just tells me where to go and where to be, and I like it that way."

"Tales of the rich and famous," Hardy said dryly. He looked good today—more casual than I was used to seeing him.

For a long time, he'd worn the stereotypical uniform of the television detective. Dark slacks, shiny loafers, button-down shirt, and tie. Over the last couple of months, he'd done away with the tie and strayed more toward pullover sweaters and such. The slacks were still in play, though I'd caught him wearing chinos a couple of times and more casual shoes. The changes suited him. All around, Hardy looked way more relaxed than I'd ever seen him.

His new way of life looked good on him.

"Yes, well," Daniel agreed, "remember, a lot of this is my family's money." He grinned. "Being a trust fund baby has its perks."

It did, but he was also a well-respected and handsomely paid author. "Don't sell yourself short. You have a signing coming up, and I know Harper and I are going to have to beat the female fans off you."

He grinned. "You give me too much credit, but I look forward to seeing you swat away my legions of adoring female fans with the bookstore's broom."

Shaking my head, I unpacked the box and carried the books back to the new safe in the back. I didn't trust the storage room anymore, not after the last case's bookstore break-ins.

When I came back to the main part of the store, Hardy and Daniel had made themselves at home on the comfy couches, both holding a cup of coffee. I waved at them and went back to the register just as the bell over the door rang again.

It had become a strange ritual between them. If they happened to come in at the same time, they'd chat with me for a while before retreating to the seating area and chatting over a cup of coffee.

It was nice if I were being honest with myself.

I greeted the customers, two women in their thirties, if I had to guess. One of them glanced Daniel's way and sucked in a gasp. Hiding my smile, I told them about the sale and let them know I was available if they had any questions.

Daniel didn't live in our town, but everyone knew he lived close by and spent time at my shop. But those were the locals who didn't give a whit about local celebrities. The tourists, which these two appeared to be, were a little more difficult. Daniel tended to stay away during the heavy tourist season to keep his privacy and to avoid a scene at my store. He told me he much preferred his days of anonymity, but life was lonely in that big ol' mansion he owned.

I kept an eye on them as they browsed the shop and would intervene if I needed to. A little starstruck look was harmless, really.

Daniel caught my eye and smiled. I rolled my eyes at him but couldn't help smiling back. Making fun of him about his star power was one of the joys of my day, and I didn't get to do it too often.

Harper poked her head out a little while later. The tourists bought a couple of books and left, but not before walking slowly past Daniel to gawk at him. I'd get a lot of mileage over this one for the next few weeks.

Harper waved me away and took her spot behind the register, so I headed over to the seating area and made myself a cup of Earl Grey.

Hardy scooted over so I could sit beside him on the two-person couch. "Discussing crime?" I asked. "Giving Daniel inspiration for new work?"

"All I have to do is read the news for inspiration," Daniel said. "We have way too much access to information these days."

Hardy laughed. "It does make things harder sometimes." He topped up the last of his coffee and stood. "I have to get back. Nice to see you as always, Dakota. Save me a copy of Daniel's book, please. I haven't given a bad review in a while now and feel very keyboard warriorish."

Daniel laughed. "You never know, Hardy. I might teach you a few things. Even old and grizzled detectives need to brush up on the basics every once in a while."

Hardy grinned, though it was a little sharper this time. "Let's hope you never need me, then." He inclined his head. "Dakota. I'll see you soon."

"Bye, Hardy."

He brushed past and headed out the door, leaving the bookstore in silence. Harper busied herself cleaning up the register area while I sipped my tea and enjoyed the reprieve.

"I'll get the rest, Harper. Go on home."

She held up the dust cloth. "You sure?"

"I'm sure." I smiled and waved her out. "The sale is finally over tomorrow, so I have to put a lot of things away. No biggie."

"If you're sure."

When I nodded, she grabbed her purse from under the register. "I'll see you tomorrow then."

"Take care." Daniel waved.

When the key turned in the lock, announcing Harper's departure, Daniel let out a long sigh.

"Uh oh. That kind of day?"

He set his mug down and crossed one ankle over his knee. "Let's talk in hypotheticals."

I stared at him over the rim of my mug. "Weird, but okay."

"I have a friend who may or may not have a stalker."

"Does this friend have dark hair and cheat at chess?"

Daniel laughed. "Hypotheticals, Dakota."

I huffed a laugh. "Fine. Usually, people who have a stalker know about it. It's not a maybe kind of thing."

"True. But this stalker might be blackmailing me."

My tea sloshed in the cup. "Blackmail?" I thought about it. "Do they have information that is damaging *and* true?"

Daniel shook his head. "One out of two."

"One is much more important than the other, legally speaking."

"Damaging, but not true," he allowed.

"Do we still have to speak in hypotheticals?" I asked.

Daniel groaned. "It's so much easier to play pretend than to admit what's happening to me."

I set my tea mug down. "That's serious. Have you contacted the police?"

He frowned. "No. I'm hoping it will blow over."

A stunned laugh burst from me. "You've been hanging out with me for a while now. Have you ever seen anything blowing over?"

He scrubbed a hand over his chin. "True." Daniel shook his head. "I'm not sure what to do."

"What do they want?"

"Money." He grimaced. "A lot of it."

"Even if you gave it to them, which I don't recommend, they'll never leave you alone."

His lips twisted. "I *am* the crime writer here, Dakota."

I had to laugh. "And if you don't give it to them?"

"They plan on launching a smear campaign against me, accusing me of plagiarizing my books."

I sucked in a gasp. "Daniel. You should have talked to Hardy about it while he was here."

He walked over to the coffeepot and emptied the rest into his glass. "Hardy won't help me."

I barked a laugh. "What? Of course he would."

Daniel's eyes flashed. "He won't. Hardy sees me as competition."

"That's ridiculous. He is an officer of the law. No matter what his personal feelings are, he is oathbound to help you."

Daniel's eyes glittered with amusement. "Oathbound?"

I waved a hand at him. "You know what I mean." My tea sat abandoned on the table, but I was too stunned to get up and refresh it. "Hardy will help you because that's who he is, regardless of how either of you feel about me."

"I would need it kept quiet."

"He's a good detective."

"I was actually thinking of something else," he mused as his gaze slid to the newest area of Tattered Pages.

I frowned. The only thing over there right now was the extra spillover area for books and the P.I. extension office.

I stilled. "Daniel. No. That's too important to be my first case."

He sat back down and studied me. "You are far too humble. Do you know people speak about you around town and how your case-solving rate is just as high as Hardy's?"

I rolled my eyes. "No self-respecting civilian would use the words 'case-solving rate' in the same sentence unless they were addicted to true crime podcasts."

Daniel's lips twitched. "Fine. I embellished a little. But your rate is as high as his."

"Impossible," I scoffed.

"Improbable. I believe Hardy arrived in town not long before you became this town's amateur sleuth."

I frowned. "Hardy wades into far more danger than I ever have."

"I'm sure he does, but you're no slouch either."

"I'd much rather be a slouch when it comes to the dangerous part," I grumbled.

Daniel stood. "I'd like this to be your first case. Figure out who it is and why I'm being targeted."

"You're being targeted because you're famous, and everyone knows you're rich."

His eyes flashed. "Everyone?" Daniel shook his head. "They assume I am, but only locals have seen where I actually live. Perhaps it's someone from Silverwood?"

I thought about it. "Makes the most sense. They knew your home address, which only locals would." I eyed him. "The house isn't in your name, is it?"

Daniel's lips curled into a smile. "See, you're already gathering clues." He shook his head. "And no, of course not. It's in a trust. My name is not on anything. Not even my car."

"Smart." I needed to think more along those lines. I'd come into an insane amount of money lately and hadn't done a thing about it other than stash it in various accounts. Technically, I was a very rich lady. Fear kept me from touching any of it.

He leaned forward. "You haven't touched any of the money," he said softly, as if he'd read my mind. I asked

Daniel to keep his access to my account while I tried to figure out what I wanted to do with it.

"No. It's overwhelming." I smiled, but I knew it didn't reach my eyes. "I've never had the kind of money where I could just up and disappear without a word and be completely fine for as long as I wanted."

His eyes softened. "It takes some getting used to. I still feel guilty when I buy something frivolous."

The mental image made me laugh. "I can just see you leaning over a Porsche, debating between it and the Honda."

Daniel chuckled. "I don't feel that guilty." He rose, taking his mug with him. "I know you need to close up, so I'll head out. Be careful going home."

I rose as well and took his mug. Daniel leaned over and brushed a kiss against my cheek. "Think about it. You need a case, and I'm a willing client who trusts you."

I touched my fingers to my cheek and swallowed hard. "I will."

Daniel winked and headed toward the door. I hurried after him to unlock it. When he was gone, I leaned against it and let out a long breath.

I might be in trouble.

TWO

Turning Pages Investigations was still in its infancy. I didn't even have a sign for the door. I also had no clue how to run a P.I. firm, but I seemed to be doing okay with all the investigations I got involved in. However, that was much different from running a business for it.

When I purchased Tattered Pages, the bookstore was already in the black. Enough for me to be comfortable with the purchase. Since books are my first love, keeping it that way wasn't difficult. Now the store was doing better than ever, and I was still in love with the place.

Poppy meowed and twined around my calves. I reached down and gave her a scratch behind the ears before scooping her up and smooching her on the back of the head.

She flicked her ears but tolerated it.

"That's the spirit." I chuckled and grabbed my purse, juggling them both as I locked up behind me.

Once I tucked Poppy into the cat hammock, and she curled into a little apostrophe, I turned the car on and blew warmth into my hands. Silverwood Hollow was beautiful at night. Soft lights lit up the shops dotting the town square area, and there was a chill in the air that made me long for autumn to hurry up and stay put.

A lot had happened during my time here, but I'd never lost my love for this place. Smiling, I flipped the dials to raise the heater temperature and settled in for the drive home.

THE NEXT MORNING, I arrived bright and early at the shop. Poppy headed straight to the back to do whatever cats did during the day. She never destroyed or broke anything but locating her when I needed her was like finding a needle in a haystack once she went deeper inside Tattered Pages.

Harper wasn't in yet, so I made coffee and a pot of tea and then straightened up the area for customers. They were split firmly between the two beverages, so I ensured I had plenty of herbal and Earl Grey stocked and kept plenty of dark roast beans around.

I'd done a thorough job of getting the store ready last night, so there wasn't too much to do. Once I had a steaming cup of coffee in my hand, I opened the expansion and stepped inside.

The scent of fresh wood hit me, and I breathed it in, smiling as I trailed my hand over the antique desk I'd purchased on a whim. I'd asked for more shelving in here, so the new space still had the same literary feel to it, but customers could tell it wasn't a true continuation of Tattered Pages. Most of the time, I kept the door between them shut.

I'd been up for a while last night thinking about Daniel and his request. I would have helped him regardless, but making this my first official P.I. case for Turning Pages sent a squirm of apprehension through me. It was one thing to help people out when they needed it. It was an entirely different thing to stake a business on my success.

If I failed before, it was no reflection of my ability. Not really. I wasn't supposed to be investigating anyway. At least according to Hardy. But now, with a contract and a retainer, and all that good stuff I had to do to officially secure a client, if I failed, it could affect my business.

Then, in the back of my mind, I always remembered the ridiculous amount of money I left untouched in my bank account, and I thought again about leaving it all behind and sunning my buns in Aruba for the rest of my days.

The thought made me laugh. I loved books more than the beach. Aruba might be fun for a week or two, but I knew soon enough I'd revert to my hobgoblin, cardigan-wearing, book-reading ways and find myself curled up, barefoot in my oversized chair, sipping on coffee and hissing at anyone who dared interrupt me during the good parts.

But Harper was excellent at running the bookstore,

and she was far too valuable to me to keep calling her an assistant. Maybe it was time to let go of some old things and embrace some new ones.

I'd never give up ownership of the store. I loved it too much.

But I could promote her, bring in another helper, and offer a raise and a percentage of the store's equity. She never asked me for much of anything, and she'd seen her fair share of craziness around me.

I let out a sigh. Yes. That felt right. Tears shimmered in my eyes.

For every ending, there was always another beginning, wasn't there?

I pulled my cell out of my pocket and dialed Daniel.

"I hope you're calling to say yes," he said in greeting.

"I am, and I wanted to talk to you about Harper. Mind popping by today?"

"Sure. I'm in between books, so I have nothing but time. How about I bring lunch?"

"Sounds great."

"Same place?"

"As long as you get me that pasta I like."

"I wouldn't dream of getting you anything else." Amusement brimmed in his voice. "See you in a few hours."

We hung up just as the bell over the door jingled.

"Dakota?" Harper called.

"In the back!"

She popped her head around the corner and waved.

"Morning." Harper handed me a paper cup from a coffee shop around the corner. I still missed the old one, but those days were long gone. The new shop had good coffee, but Trudy had a magic touch with such things.

I plucked the stopper out of the drink and took a sip.

"Pumpkin spice," Harper said. "It's pretty good."

She missed the other shop as much, if not more, than I did. Harper leaned against the doorframe, a thoughtful look on her face.

"Oh no. I know that look."

She laughed. "I know you just expanded, but have you ever thought about serving coffee here?"

I jerked my head toward the makeshift coffee bar we already had. "Cheap, easy, effective."

Harper snorted. "Real coffee."

I gently waved my latte at her. "This is not real coffee. If we wanted to be real snobs about it, we could call this a travesty."

"Pumpkin spice is life," she said, rolling her eyes at me. "We don't have to go all out at first. Maybe just lattes and regular coffee."

"We'd have to hire a barista."

Harper shrugged. "I think it would pay for itself pretty quickly."

I motioned for her to come inside. Once she was in, I shut the door and pulled a chair out. "I'm glad you brought that up. There's something I've wanted to talk to you about."

Harper winced. "Uh oh. Am I overstepping?" She set

her coffee on the desk and tucked a stray strand of blonde hair behind her ear.

"No. Not at all." I sat down and clasped my hands together. "You've been with me for a long time now, and things haven't been exactly..." My voice trailed off.

"Normal?"

I gave her a sheepish smile. "Exactly. I guess it's not every day your boss runs around trying to catch murderers."

My assistant laughed. "I'd say not. I'm not complaining. I learned a lot from you, but I learned a lot on my own, too. Before we go any further, I want to say I love working here."

"It's nothing bad, I promise." I remembered every time my boss said she wanted to talk, my mind whirled with all the ways it could go wrong.

Harper slumped with relief. "Oh good. You had me worried for a minute."

"It's good news, actually." I winced. "I hope."

"Okay." Harper studied me. "I'm nervous again."

"Please don't be. As you can see, I remodeled the shop in the hopes of opening a P.I. firm."

"Yes," she said slowly. "And you've been hesitating for weeks."

I grimaced. "I don't want to fail."

Harper tilted her head. "I've never seen you fail at anything you've put your mind to. Why would this be any different?"

The vote of confidence warmed my heart. "I have no

idea how to be a true P.I. And, technically, I can't be one yet. I still have to take my polygraph and get my finger-prints taken."

Harper's lips pursed. "So go get them done."

An exasperated sigh broke from me. "I have an appointment next week."

"Alright," she said with a chuckle. "Just making sure you're not dragging your feet too much."

"If business goes well, I won't be able to do as much around the store."

Harper nodded, a gleam sparkling in her eyes. "Am I getting another raise? I definitely won't argue about that."

"Not quite," I hedged.

Harper's brows lifted. "Then I have no idea what this is about."

"I'd like to promote you to manager, and I'd like to bring on two more helpers so you can take more time off. You'd go from hourly to salary, and I'd also like to offer you an equity package."

Harper blinked. Her mouth opened, then snapped shut. "Uh," she said.

I smiled. "You can think about it. I'll have to put the paperwork together, but I should have it by this evening. Check your email around seven."

"Two people?" she asked hoarsely.

"Two," I confirmed. "I've needed help for a while now, and you deserve time off."

She picked up her latte and took a sip. "Moving from

hourly to salary will be comparable to what I'm making now?"

"I can understand the concern, but there's nothing for you to worry about. You can do the math when you get the paperwork, but I assure you, I plan to ensure you're well compensated for your new role."

"And the new duties will be in the paperwork as well?"

I'd written those up a while ago. "Of course."

Harper slowly nodded. She seemed like she was in shock. "Can I help pick the people?"

I smiled at her. "You can do more than that. I'll hand over the entire process if you want it."

She grinned at me. "My answer, barring any surprises in the paperwork, is yes."

I laughed. "I promise I'll have someone better in math than I am double-checking the numbers."

Harper nodded and stood, taking her coffee. "Thank you so much," she breathed. "I won't let you down."

"You never have. I don't expect you to start now."

She hurried out of the expansion, leaving me smiling after her.

Now, I had to figure out how to properly compensate someone for their invaluable impact on my shop.

HARPER TOOK an extra hour for lunch to run some personal errands, beaming on her way out the door. Daniel popped in a little while later, holding a large bag of take-out. I flipped the sign to *Out to Lunch* and locked the door.

"Mmm," I said as the scent of garlic and herbs trailed behind him.

"I'm starting to think you only like me for my takeout," he said as he set the bags down on the table in the seating area.

"I like you for many reasons, but I can't lie. The takeout is the main one."

Daniel grinned. "I'm glad we're finally being truthful." He pulled out a round takeout container and flourished like he was at a fancy restaurant. "Your pasta, mademoiselle."

I sank onto the couch and took it, holding it up to my nose. "I'm glad we only eat there once a week. If it were any more, you'd have to roll me to the couch."

Daniel took his out—lasagna, more than likely—then passed the breadsticks over. I took only one. Carb on top of carb on top of carb. Yum, but I might be good for nothing once I finished.

When we had everything out and Daniel had settled into the seat opposite me, I leaned forward. "I'd like to run something by you."

His eyes glittered. "Intrigue. I like it."

I laughed. "Not quite. I need a competitive compensation package for Harper."

"You're finally promoting that poor girl?"

I snorted and tossed a salt packet at him. "She's the highest-paid shop assistant in three counties, and you know it!"

"Yes, but she's the only one with a murder-solving boss.

That has to be terrible on the blood pressure."

I rolled my eyes. "Are you going to help me or not?"

"Of course I'll help. What do you want to offer?"

Daniel and I batted ideas back and forth for the next forty-five minutes, and by the time we finished eating, I had a good idea on what I wanted to do for Harper.

Satisfied, I stood and started cleaning up our mess. Daniel helped, and when we finished, he sat back down.

"Should we talk about my case?"

I groaned and put my hand over my swollen belly. "I am not official yet. I have to do my polygraph and get my fingerprints taken care of. In two weeks, I should have everything ready to go."

Daniel nodded. "So we can't do a contract until you're officially licensed. No problem. We can discuss the issue and devise a plan to figure out who's behind it. Once that's all settled, your paperwork should be finalized."

"I'll send you over the contract I came up with. If everything looks good, we can sign it once I'm official." I held up a finger. "Wait a moment. Let me get my notebook."

Daniel stood to get himself a cup of coffee while I ran back to the desk. When I came back, a steaming mug of coffee sat on the table in front of my seat.

"Thanks!"

Daniel sipped from his mug. "No serious discussions should take place without food or beverage."

"I agree." Clicking my pen, I opened the notebook to the first page. "Tell me everything."

THREE

I skimmed over my notes, shaking my head as I tried to make sense of everything Daniel had told me. There were more suspects than I expected, although I should have. I'd temporarily forgotten how famous Daniel was.

Groaning, I set the notebook aside for now and stood to stretch my sore muscles.

Daniel would be at the store signing books in a few weeks—if we found his blackmailer.

And that was as big if. According to Daniel, the publishing business could be cutthroat, and the competition fierce. He'd had ideas stolen before and now kept everything close to the vest, even going so far as to write the book and then send it out to his agent, without giving her anything except a one to two sentence concept. Fortunately for him, he was at the point in his career where he could do that.

If someone launched a smear campaign against him

right before the release, it could ruin his career and tank the book before it ever had the chance to get off the ground.

I didn't have long to get my license and solve this case.

He'd written me an overly large advance check, which I tried to refuse multiple times.

"Dakota," he said patiently when I pushed it back for the third time. "You are providing me a service. I'm your first customer. It's a new business, and you should separate these funds from your other ones."

I knew he was right, so I begrudgingly accepted it. It would hurt his feelings if I didn't cash it, so I tucked it into my purse and made a mental note to stop at the bank on the way home this evening.

I had a couple of people at the top of my list. One was an ex-girlfriend who just found out he was living in the area. The next was an author friend he made at a critique group. The girlfriend wasn't a long-lived relationship, but it was long enough that I thought his worry had merit. Six months wasn't something to sneeze at. The critique group relationship quickly soured, and the budding author swore vengeance on not just Daniel but the entire group of twelve. That one was less worthy but still worth checking out.

The others were a new editor Daniel started working with on his latest book, though even he questioned the merit of it. I thought he was being paranoid, but he'd given me a quelling look and said something along the lines of,

"Dakota, I write murder for a living. Of course, I'm paranoid."

He also had a fan who'd taken quite the shine to his work. Daniel didn't think much of it initially, but once the fan started sending him daily emails that had grown increasingly threatening and erratic, he had to block the emails and file a police report.

I had a few more on the list, but those were the most promising, at least from him. There were a couple I added after he left. One was an aspiring author who asked way too many questions about Daniel and his work. Prying questions that I stopped answering months ago. I didn't think too much of it. When people loved a book, they could get a little intense about it.

Now that this was happening, I added her to ensure I paid closer attention the next time she came into the shop.

I closed the notebook and tucked it into my purse. The day had gotten away from me, and dusk was settling over the town. Today was a slow day for customers, so it wouldn't be a big deal to close up early.

"Poppy?" I called as I double-checked the locks on the expansion and headed out into the main area.

Her collar jingled as she rounded the corner. I switched it out a few weeks ago because she'd figured out if she popped out around a corner while I was in the shop, it would scare the bejeezus out of me. Even though I knew Poppy was only a cat, she'd done some borderline super-natural things during the time I had her.

She quickly figured out she was scaring me, so I had to

deal with her popping out like a cat serial killer at least once per hour. The first time I spilled hot tea on myself, I marched myself down to the pet store and bought her the bell.

She held a grudge for weeks over it.

"Ready?"

She meowed at me which I took as a yes. "Come on then." I tapped the desk. With one quick leap, she sat before me. I scratched her under the chin and scooped her up. "Let's go home."

She meowed again in agreement.

Once I settled at the table with my leftovers, I pulled my laptop over and started doing deep dives on all the subjects I could. The aspiring author was much more difficult. With a name like Jane White, I'd be in the search engine weeds forever. She might be the most difficult to track down, so I stuck her at the back of the list and started with Daniel's list first.

Alice Merritt was the easiest to get information on. Someone needed to sit that girl down and show her exactly how easy it was for someone to get information about them when you had lax security. Most of her social media posts were public. She had pictures from work and home easily accessible to anyone, as well as her birthday listed, including the year, and her middle name.

"Oh, Alice," I breathed. She was pretty. Slim, blonde, brown-eyed, and claimed to work in the legal field several towns over. Daniel said they'd met during a book signing.

When I'd given him the side-eye over that info, he'd laughed and sworn she was the only one.

I wasn't sure I believed him, but I gave him the benefit of the doubt.

There was nothing too concerning with her postings. Most were pictures of her out with friends or decorative quote memes. Her relationship status was listed as complicated, which was a little curious if she was talking about Daniel. He told me they'd broken up a few months ago and hadn't spoken to her since.

There'd been no animosity between them over the breakup, though he said he was the instigator, and Alice had no desire to sever the relationship. I hoped that was the case because the last thing I wanted was to get too involved in Daniel's personal life.

During a lull in the search, my email dinged with a message from him. He'd sent back Harper's contract with a few notes. I skimmed the message and opened the attachment with the notes. When no obvious red flags jumped out at me, I made the changes he requested, did a final proof, and emailed it to Harper with a note asking her to get back to me by the end of the week.

When that was finished, I closed the laptop and got up to pour myself a glass of wine.

If Harper took the job, I could slide a lot of work off my plate. She'd need training on some of the more technical aspects of running a business, but Harper was nothing if not a fast learner. I had zero reservations she'd pick things up quickly.

As much as I loved that, it made me nervous. What if I couldn't get this P.I. business off the ground?

And then I had to think, did it really matter? I was so used to managing my money with a semi-tight hand, but I no longer had to do that.

I could relax.

The thought of that made my shoulders tense.

Laughing at myself, I took my glass of wine and sank onto my couch, flipping on the television when I settled in.

I'd reached my daily quota of thinking.

Now it was time for brain rot.

FOUR

Bright and early the next morning, I pulled into the print shop to pick up the signs announcing Daniel's signing. He gave me free rein on the design but asked me to allow him to see it before I paid to have it printed.

I obliged, and he didn't ask for a single tweak to the design, which made me feel warm and fuzzy. He had the power of a big marketing department behind him, so for him to allow me this amount of leeway with an event made me feel good about my design skills while also wondering in the back of my mind if this was because he was sweet on me.

Then I had to crush that self-doubt because Daniel had an incredible head for business, and he wouldn't allow something that made him or his books look bad.

My arms were full when I bustled into the shop. Harper opened this morning and waved at me with her coffee cup before hurrying to help.

"What's all this?" she asked, taking half my burden.

"The Jensen signing." I had two for the window and one large, banner-style sign I planned to put by the new release display.

"I haven't read anything he's written in the last year," Harper confessed, laughing at my horror-stricken look. She shrugged. "Crime isn't really my thing. I prefer lighter, fluffier rom-coms and cozy books."

"We all have our favorites. Though maybe give the newest one a whirl because we have him graciously agreeing to do a signing here." Daniel could go anywhere, and people would fall all over themselves to get him to sign at their stores. I didn't even bring it up because I didn't want him to feel like I was abusing our friendship.

When he did, he could have blown me over with a feather. I jumped at the opportunity because I'm not a fool, but with the caveat that I didn't want him doing this because of our relationship and only if he really wanted to.

He'd laughed for a straight five minutes.

I had a small bookshop in a small town. Of course he was doing this because we were friends. Even if he wouldn't say it out loud. So I decided I'd do the biggest social media blitz I'd ever been involved in. Everyone in the state was going to know who we had signing here even if it killed me.

While we had a lull in customers, Harper and I busied ourselves with setting everything up. It was weird to see Daniel's face plastered all over the shop, considering I saw it at least twice a week in person.

The bell rang, and Hardy stepped in, an odd look on his face.

"Everything okay, Detective?" Harper asked, amusement twinkling in her eyes.

"Do I have to see his face every time I walk past your shop?" Hardy said in greeting.

I laughed. "Just until the signing is over."

He sighed and shook his head. "What are the odds you can sell me one of the books he brought you?"

I winced. "I'll ask him, but I'm pretty sure I'm not allowed to sell any of the stock until the release day." A thought occurred to me. "Though I can let you borrow the copy he gave me if you promise to give it back to me."

"Of course I will," he agreed.

I held up a finger. "Let me grab it." Hurrying away, I left him with Harper while I went to the office to grab the one Daniel had given me before he'd brought that box to me. When I handed it over, Hardy flipped it open, eyes darkening when he saw the inscription.

I'd forgotten about that. It was innocent, but it implied an intimacy between us.

To Harper. A friend and a not-so formidable chess partner. I bet YouTube has remedial videos that might help. - Daniel

The inscription made me laugh, and I vowed once again to catch him cheating.

"It's really good," I said, hoping to draw his attention away from it. "You'll never guess who the killer is."

Hardy smiled. "Bet you I can."

"Ten bucks says you won't."

He tilted his head. "Dakota Adair. I wouldn't have taken you for a betting woman."

"I read at least a book a week. There are few book crimes I haven't guessed before the reveal. Ten bucks. Scout's honor. No lying." I stuck out my hand.

Hardy placed his hand in mine, and we shook. "Deal." He tucked it under his arm. "I have to run. Thanks for this. I'll have it back in a week if that's okay."

"Perfectly fine. Don't let anyone else borrow it."

"I wouldn't dream of it." Hardy winked and headed out of the shop.

Harper sighed. "You sure you don't want to get back together with him? He looks at you like..." She shook her head. "Like the sun has finally come out after a long day of rain."

I blinked in surprise and cleared my throat. "It's uh..."

She held up her hand. "Complicated. Right. I know." Harper shook her head. "I'm just saying, I'd give my left foot for half a look like that." She glided away to the back, leaving me standing there befuddled.

"Right," I said faintly. "I'll keep that in mind."

Later that afternoon, the aspiring author/intense fan on my suspect list showed up. She was younger, not too long out of college if I had to guess, and carried herself like she didn't want to be noticed. I smiled when she walked in and tried not to read too much into her behavior.

She wore her usual skinny jeans, high-top sneakers, a

tank top and a hoodie over it. No makeup and she kept her hair in a high ponytail.

I dealt with a lot of writers in my line of work and the range of personalities was a little wild. Most of the ones I met were painfully introverted. She seemed like this, so I was polite, but I tried not to bother her too much when she was browsing.

Daniel was introverted but possessed a natural charisma that hid it. He could navigate a crowd with ease and carry a conversation.

This girl could barely make eye contact and spoke mostly in mumbles.

"Hello, Jane," I greeted her.

She flicked her hand up in a wave but quickly lowered it back to her side as if she were uncomfortable with even that much acknowledgment. "*A Time for Murder.* Do you have it yet?"

I shook my head. "Sorry. It won't be available until the release day."

Jane frowned. "But I saw Daniel come in with a big box."

My stomach clenched. "Oh? When did you see that?"

She shrugged. "Yesterday or something. Maybe the day before. Was that box full of books? It looked like it was."

I had to be polite but firm. "We have a lot of deliveries during the week, Jane. Any copies of *A Time for Murder* we receive are kept under lock and key. We'd get into a lot of trouble with a publisher if we released the author's books before we were allowed to. I'm sure you understand."

From the look on her face, she most definitely did not understand. "But I want to buy one."

I smiled politely. "Mr. Jensen has many fans who want an early copy of his book, but we can't accommodate anyone who asks."

Her expression turned thunderous. "I bet he gave you one."

My polite smile turned frosty. "As a long-time bookseller, I receive many advance reading copies from many genres and publishers."

She didn't like that answer. Jane dropped her eyes and scuffed her shoe along my well-polished floor. "Well, let me borrow it."

This young woman was about to go to the top of my list if she didn't cool it. "I am also not authorized to give out advanced copies of any books Tattered Pages receives." Pot meet kettle, considering I just gave Hardy my copy. "If you're interested in procuring one, you're always welcome to look into the publisher's program to see if they allow interested readers to acquire them."

She opened her mouth to speak again, but I'd had enough. I leaned into her space. "Is there anything else, Jane? My answer to anything involving an early copy of Mr. Jensen's book is a resounding no. Please do not ask me again."

Her eyes flashed with annoyance. "No," she mumbled.

"Then you're welcome to browse the store to find

something else you might be interested in. Otherwise, I hope you have a wonderful day."

Jane's brows drew together. Anger flickered over her face before she turned around and stomped out of the store.

Harper let out a whoosh of breath. "She's awful."

I shook my head. "I can't tell if she's naturally disagreeable, or if she's just obsessed with Daniel in a very unhealthy way."

"Who says she can't be both?" Harper grumbled.

I laughed and turned away from the door. "Let's hope we don't see her again for a while." Getting Daniel's books out of the shop turned into a major priority. I couldn't risk someone getting in and taking those.

"Her mother isn't anything like her," Harper said, surprising me.

"You know her?"

She shrugged. "No. Well. Not really. I know her mother. She comes to a spin class I teach down at the local gym."

I blinked at her. "You're an instructor there?"

"It's a new thing." She grinned at me. "Though I don't think I'll keep doing it with the potential new job duties coming my way."

"You saw the paperwork?"

She nodded eagerly. "I don't need a few days."

"Oh?"

"I'm happy to start right away. I just need to sign them?"

"That's all. It will take a couple of weeks to get your pay all straightened out, and we'd need to start on the new employee hunt right away."

Harper's face brightened. "Oh! I have one person in mind. She's the daughter of the owner of that new coffee shop."

I grimaced. "If we hire her, we can't talk about their coffee behind their back anymore."

Harper snickered. "We probably shouldn't do it even if we don't hire her."

"Wise," I agreed. "But we still will, right?"

"Oh yes, we will. I thought it was impossible to mess up a pumpkin spice latte."

I chuckled. "Let's hope they're getting their feet under them and going through some growing pains. I'll give them another chance in a week or so."

Harper sighed. "Yeah. I miss Trudy. Her coffee creations were magic."

"Me too," I agreed. "Maybe they have a specialty coffee that we haven't had yet. I need to stop by the place and look at their official menu."

"I think this might be one of those things where they saw an opening in the market and tried to capitalize on it."

"If it is, it won't last for long."

Harper tapped her nails on the desk. "Which is why we should definitely think about starting a little coffee bar..."

I hoped she was just as eager about the bookstore as she was about the potential of a coffee bar inside it. "Hold your horses. Let's see how they do first. I don't want to pull business away while they're still working things out."

She sighed and sank into the chair. "You're right. And a better person than I am."

"Not at all, but being a small business owner is tough, especially in the first few years. They won't make it if they aren't in it for the right reasons, though. The community is too tight knit to allow it."

"You're right. But if they don't get it together soon, I will have to go for my fix in the next town over."

We had a few businesses ebb and flow over the last year or so. The economy hadn't quite bounced back from a few years ago, and more and more people were cutting out unnecessary expenses. Fortunately, hardcore readers considered us a necessary expense, so we hadn't had as rough of a ride as others. Another coffee shop went under after Trudy's, and this one popped up not too long after.

I was content not to pay five bucks for a syrup-laden latte, but sometimes, especially during fall, there was nothing like the first sip of a fall-spiced sugary latte.

Making them at home never tasted the same, but I suspected it had more to do with the ingredients than it did my skills. If I could get my hands on the same things the bigger coffee shops used to make their coffee, I had no doubt I could save quite a few bucks making them myself.

But no one wanted to give up their trade secrets. My next move was to try out YouTube and see how some of the foodies made theirs.

Or...someone with mad barista skills could open a new

place, or the one we already had could find an amazing one.

"Dakota?"

I laughed. "Sorry. I started thinking about homemade pumpkin spice lattes and got into the weeds a little."

Harper held her hands up. "Not me. Take my money. The syrups they use are all sticky, and I don't have the right coffee machine. I'd rather pay someone to do it all for me."

"Normally I don't mind if it tastes like Trudy's used to. But until we get someone on that level again, I'm going to tackle mine at home."

The shop phone rang. I was closest to it, so I picked it up.

"Tattered Pages, this is Dakota."

A strange, digitally altered voice spoke. "Cancel the Jensen signing. If you don't, you'll regret it."

I stilled. "Excuse me?"

"You heard me. Cancel his signing. He's nothing but a copycat."

"I happen to know Mr. Jenkins very well, and I think you're wrong."

Tension simmered over the line. "What if I can prove it?"

"Then prove it. I won't cave to anonymous threats from people making outlandish accusations without firm proof."

"You'll do what I tell you to!" the voice shouted. "Or I'll—I'll—"

"Yes?" I said. "You'll what?"

The person hung up. I stared at the phone for a long time before stepping away.

"Dakota? Everything okay?"

"Someone wants me to cancel Daniel's signing."

She snorted. "On what grounds?"

"He's been fielding accusations of plagiarism."

Her eyes widened. "No. I refuse to believe it."

Me too. "I don't think it's true. He asked for assistance figuring out who it is."

"Ah." Harper nodded. "I figured it was something like that."

"I may call Hardy and loop him in, but I'll have to ask Daniel first."

"How can he help?"

"I'm not a detective and have never handled a case like this. Usually, I stumble into things later. This all just started happening, and I don't know anyone involved except for him. Hardy may have insight I don't."

The bell jingled. I smiled and waved at the newest customer. "I'm going to the office to do some bookkeeping. Next week, I'll show you how to maintain them. For the first six months, I'll double-check all your work just to ensure everything is in order, but after that, I'll turn you loose."

Harper nodded. "Thanks, Dakota. I'll close up shop soon and pop in when I'm finished."

I gave her a grateful smile and went off to tackle the books.

FIVE

I called Daniel on the way home and told him what happened. He blew out a heavy breath.

"I was afraid of that. After not being receptive to their demands, I'm not surprised they tried to put pressure on you."

When I relayed what happened with his fan, he groaned. "Thank you for not selling any of those."

I patted the box next to me. "They're no longer in the shop. I have them in the car with me. No one is getting their hands on them."

Daniel sighed. "This feels like déjà vu, except those books aren't worth millions."

"Says you. Do you know how much I could get for these on the black market?"

Amusement came over the line. "Yes, well, I suppose I could see you slinging illegal books in a dark alley."

"I've gone to the dark side."

"On a serious note, if this gets too dangerous, I want you to promise me you'll step away."

"This is the first time I think I can confidently say it has not gotten too dangerous. I haven't found a single body."

"It's a sad state of affairs when you find that statement comforting."

I pulled into the driveway and turned the car off. "Oh! Before I forget, are you okay with me sharing some of these details with Hardy?"

"As long as he doesn't get too much into my business."

"I'll keep that in mind. I'm mostly concerned about the phone call at the shop today."

"If it's any consolation, things like this ramp up with every release. Everything will die down in a month or so."

I made sure to lock the front door behind me. "You do this every single time?"

"Unfortunately, though, this is the first time someone has resorted to blackmail."

"Did something escalate recently? Were there any incidents, even small ones, that could have triggered the accusations?"

"I thought the same thing. My best answer is not recently. Something happened at my last book signing, but it was eighteen months ago. I'd put it out of my mind a long time ago."

"It could be nothing but better safe than sorry."

"I signed a book for a young woman, and she didn't like the inscription. We had a line out the door and had no time to do personalized autographs." He paused for a long moment. "She caused a scene, and we had to contact the local police."

"Did you ever hear from her again?"

"No. Never again."

I thought about it. "I'll jot it down in my notebook when I get home, but I'm not sure it's important."

"Did you send the paperwork to Harper?"

"I did. I now have a brand-new manager. Thanks for the help with the contract."

"Any time, Dakota."

We said our goodbyes, and I headed straight to the bedroom to put comfortable clothes on.

I was settling in to eat dinner when a knock on the door sounded. Odd. No one came by at this time of night without calling first.

Tugging my cardigan closer around me, I padded barefoot to the front door and looked through the peephole.

There was no one there.

Weird.

I looked through the curtain to the side of the door and saw a manila envelope on the front porch.

There was no way I was going to open the door now. Way too many things had happened to women who lived alone and opened the door to grab something off the porch.

Even though I was curious, my hard-won cautious

nature won out. I returned to the table to finish my dinner. Whatever it was, it could wait.

An hour later, once I was completely sure no one was lingering around the house, I opened the door and snatched the envelope up, hurrying back inside the house and locking the door behind me.

The envelope had my first and last name on it and nothing else.

I pressed it but felt nothing. Whatever it was seemed to be only paper.

Holding it away from my face, I opened it with a pair of scissors and turned it over to shake the contents out. A small bundle of papers tumbled out, tied with a piece of twine.

There was a small note tucked into the twine that said only, *Proof.*

"Hmm."

I took it over to the table in the living room and started going through everything, unconvinced this would have any legitimacy.

The first part was stapled together and labeled *A Time to Kill.* The second was also stapled together and consisted of multiple emails from Daniel to someone named *scribe1564.*

I read through the emails first but didn't see anything too concerning. Daniel was involved in a mentoring rela-tionship with a group of young writers. One, the person with the scribe email, seemed to branch off from the group and demanded more one-on-one time from Daniel.

From what I could tell, he reacted appropriately and requested they stick to his office hours. The person reacted poorly to this and insisted their work was better than the other group members, so they deserved more time.

By the time I waded through all that nonsense, I felt a stirring sense of sympathy for Daniel, and a strong dislike for the scribe character.

Sighing, I opened the second small stack of papers, my eyes skimming down the first page until I stilled and sat up straight, my heart pounding in my chest.

The first page was almost identical to Daniel's first page.

How could that be?

I flipped to the second page and kept reading, thinking surely it was a mistake, but no. The second and third were close to identical.

How did this person get access to Daniel's manuscript? But a nagging thought crossed my mind, one I didn't even want to ask myself.

If this wasn't Daniel's, was he guilty of the accusations against him? And if he was, what was I going to do about it?

Disgusted, I pushed the papers away like they were a cockroach.

He was my friend, maybe eventually more than one, but if this were true, there was no way I could continue seeing him.

But, if that were true, why in the world would he hire

me to tackle this for him? That wasn't something someone guilty would do.

Unless he was trying to shift the blame to someone else.

I rubbed my hands over my face and groaned. My brain hurt.

Tomorrow, I'd take everything to the office and try to make sense of it all.

SIX

Hardy brought coffee the next morning. I breathed a sigh of relief when I realized it was from the next town over, and he'd kept it warm inside a thermal cup.

"Oooh," I breathed when he handed it to me. "And you kept it piping hot? Thank you so much."

"I'd rather have no coffee than cold coffee."

"That makes two of us."

The shop wasn't open yet. Harper would be in to work in about half an hour, so Hardy and I could talk without fear of being interrupted. "Want to come to the new office with me?"

"Lead the way."

He smelled good, like fresh air and citrus, and looked even better. "You look nice today," I said as I led him back to the expanded area. I looked over my shoulder. "Got a date or something?"

I said it as a joke, but when his cheeks turned pink, my

stomach dropped to my feet, and it took everything I had to keep my expression perfectly pleasant.

"Ah," I said. "Well, that's great news!" I smiled and held the door, but Hardy took it from me and motioned for me to walk ahead.

"I thought it might be time," he said.

Blood rushed through my ears, and I kept my back to him until I was sure the tears forming in my eyes were thoroughly reabsorbed. I pulled out a seat for him and settled behind my desk.

"Who's the lucky lady?" I asked.

Hardy stared at me before exhaling. "Let's not do this, Dakota. Please."

My smile froze. "Do what?"

"You don't want to know who I'm going out with as much as I don't want to tell you, so please, let's just...talk. You called me for a reason, so let's keep it to that."

My face burned with humiliation. I wanted to say so many things but couldn't form the words, so I nodded and cleared my throat. "I—I just want you to be happy." It was true. I had no right to pretend I had a claim on him when I was the one who broke us apart. Acting like he was doing something wrong was an unfair thing to do. "I'm sorry, Hardy."

His blue eyes flashed with an emotion I couldn't identify. "I'm sorry, too."

Silence fell. When I couldn't take it anymore, I took a sip of my coffee and pushed the paper packet over to him.

"I wanted to ask you some questions about how you operate, if that's okay."

Hardy's brow furrowed. "You want to ask me about detective work?" His lips curved in a smile. "You never have before. Why now?" His long, tanned fingers pulled the sheath of papers over. He flipped through them, lips tightening as he must have realized what they were.

"Daniel has a stalker of some sort. He's being blackmailed."

Hardy's attention jerked from the papers to me.

"I received an odd call at the shop yesterday demanding we cancel his signing. They said they had proof, so I asked for it. I never thought they would send anything."

"How did they send this to you?"

"They dropped it on my front porch last night."

Hardy swore. "Dakota. They know where you live?"

I nodded. "Apparently so. But it's a small town. A lot of people know where I live."

"You think they're local?" His blue eyes were piercing. Hardy's fingers tapped a sporadic rhythm on my desk.

"If they aren't, I guess this is a lot worse then, huh?"

He leaned back in his chair and studied me. "I knew he'd put you in danger one day."

I blinked in surprise. "Hardy, I—"

"His lifestyle invites it. That party we went to...all of those people there. The upper crust of society. I saw this coming from a mile away."

"That's unfair," I said quietly. "I've known Daniel for a

long time now, and he threw that party for me. Not because he wanted to."

He ignored me. "All that money you came into—" He bit his words off. "I think you should turn him down."

"I'm in no danger."

"You are *always* in danger!" he snapped.

The room went quiet. I struggled with what to say next. This was one of the main reasons Hardy and I hadn't worked, though he'd gotten much better about it when we were dating. "Daniel is my friend, Hardy. I would do the same for you."

He stood abruptly. "The difference between me and Daniel Jensen is I would never ask you to."

Hardy turned and stalked away.

My shoulders slumped and the bell jangled a discordant tune as Hardy flung open the door and left.

"Well, that went well," I muttered.

Poppy poked her orange head around the corner and meowed at me. "Yeah. He's a little angry," I murmured. The cat hopped on the desk, something she normally never did, and bumped my forehead with hers. I stroked her behind the ears. "What do you think? Is Daniel capable of stealing someone else's work? Is he a fraud?"

Poppy sat on her haunches and stared at me, silent as the grave.

"Yeah," I said with a sigh. "I don't know either." My gut said no, but I was biased when it came to him. He'd always gone out of his way to do things for me, and he'd been a wise and stalwart friend. If I couldn't trust him, who could I trust?

I buried my head in my hands and groaned. Today was starting off on the wrong foot.

It took a few hours for me to put Hardy out of my mind. My heart hurt for more than one reason. He was moving on—something he was entitled to do. I knew that odd little friendship we had would have to end, but I didn't expect it to happen so quickly. It was selfish of me to assume I'd have Hardy as a good friend forever. I wasn't naïve enough to believe things wouldn't change when he started dating again.

Any new woman in his life would not like him hanging around an ex-girlfriend. I was a fool for even entertaining it.

I had to put some distance between us for everyone's good. This was only a date. It could fizzle out immediately, or it could go on to be something for him. It didn't matter which way it went. My behavior toward him had been inappropriate, and I vowed to do better.

Even if it felt like my heart was breaking into a thousand pieces, I had to let him go.

Harper waved me away when I offered to help, telling me she was the manager now, and she decreed the boss, aka me, needed to take more time off to get the other business going.

With the incriminating papers tucked into my bag, I obliged her and left, turning my car away from the town square and toward Cole's office. There was only so much I could do on my laptop. I needed additional help that couldn't come from Hardy.

Cole Gardener had the build of an Olympic swimmer and the face of a model. He also had the dating history of a celebrity. Every time I thought he was going to settle down, I'd spot him out with a new woman on his arm. It got to the point where I stopped asking about his new girlfriends. He rarely kept them around long enough for me to get to know them.

I knocked on the doorjamb, smiling when he spotted me. He wore a pair of charcoal slacks, black loafers, and a black mock turtleneck. His hair was the same sandy blond shade but mussed like he'd been running his fingers through it. Bright green eyes were highlighted by a pair of round tortoiseshell glasses perched on his nose.

"Dakota! What a surprise." He waved me inside.

We normally tried to do lunch regularly, but he'd been busier than normal and cagy when I asked him what he was working on. "Something big," was all he would say.

"Hey, Cole." I shut the door and sat down on the small couch beside it. Cole rose from his seat and joined me.

"Coffee?"

"Just had some but thank you. How's everything going?"

"Busy still, but I'm close to the end. How about you? How's the new P.I. firm?"

I frowned. "Got my first case. That's actually why I'm here."

Cole's eyes brightened. "A mystery. I love it. What do you have for me?"

"Well, we have to talk off the record."

He placed a hand over his heart. "Why must you wound me so?"

I snickered. "Promise me."

"I promise," he said begrudgingly. "It must be important."

"It's about Daniel Jensen."

"The author?"

I nodded. Cole and Daniel had orbited each other by hanging around me, but they weren't friends. "He has a new release soon and a signing at the shop."

He crossed his arms over his chest and sat back, studying me. "Did he kill anyone?"

A laugh cracked from me. "No! Cole!"

He shrugged, his bright eyes dancing. "You have a knack for murder, darling Dakota."

"Ugh. I do not have a knack for it. You make me sound like a serial killer. If there's any knack, it's finding bodies. That's all."

"Yes," he said somberly. "That's so much better."

I belly laughed. "Stop."

"What is it then? What did the darling of the literary world do that has you wearing that concerned look?"

I pulled the paper packet from my bag and handed it to him. "Daniel approached me about a potential stalker he wanted me to investigate. Someone is blackmailing him right before his next release, saying that if he doesn't pay them a large sum, they will claim he plagiarized his latest novel."

Cole winced. "An accusation like that is a career killer."

"Exactly."

"And what is this I'm holding?" He waved the papers at me.

"Something someone claims are proof of the accusations."

Cole whistled low. "You think it's legitimate?"

I shrugged. "I can't say. Part of me thinks there's no way he could do this. He's highly intelligent and articulate, and he's always been very good to me."

Cole made a mmm noise. "And he's quite into you if the rumblings around town are to be listened to."

I snorted. "They are not," I said primly. "He has expressed interest, but he's always been a perfect gentleman around me."

"Uh huh," Cole said. "And why have you not gone out with him?"

My cheeks flushed. "That has nothing to do with this."

Cole grinned. "I'm afraid that's where you're wrong. When you're in a business like I am, you have to look at all the angles. If someone is blackmailing him, you need to find the reason why. Has someone seen his interest and wants to stop it before it goes any further? Did he anger someone? Is there professional jealousy involved? Many things could cause blackmail, but until you figure out the why, it's hard to figure out the who."

"I really don't think it's me," I grumbled.

"I think you need to rule it out," Cole said, fingers flipping through the pages.

"And how would I do that?"

Cole chuckled. "You go out with him. Publicly. And you keep your eyes and ears open for anything that feels off."

"That sounds easier said than done."

He leaned forward, bright eyes sparkling. "And you hire someone else to watch as well. It's much easier for a third party the potential stalker is unaware of to spot something off. You'll be paranoid and think it's everyone, but a professional would know what to look for."

I frowned. "I don't know any professionals."

He gasped in mock outrage. "How dare you? I am a professional and need a break from my current case. I would be ecstatic to act as an invisible third wheel for your fake date with a famous author."

I grimaced. "You want us to be bait."

"It's easy bait. No one has died yet, and you'll be in a public space at all times."

"That is not as comforting as I think you mean it to be."

"It's an easy way to figure out if the stalker is merely cyber or if it's someone physically following him."

I didn't like the idea, but Cole had a point. "I'll run it by Daniel. Do you want to come alone, or do you have someone to bring?"

"I'll ask Charlotte to come."

I waved a hand. "I do not know her, nor do I want to."

Cole laughed. "She's a colleague." He stood. "Come, and I'll introduce you. I still think you need to make more friends in this town, and I think you'll like her."

He put the papers in a drawer and led me down the hall, stopping at an office similar to his. "Charlotte?"

A feminine voice called for him to come in. I stepped into a tastefully decorated office, one full wall littered with certificates, degrees, and awards.

"This is Dakota Adair. She runs a bookshop in town."

"Tattered Pages!" Charlotte stood and offered her hand.

She was tall and pretty, with shoulder-length blonde hair and hazel eyes. Her smile was wide and friendly, and she was dressed smartly but not overly professional.

"Nice to meet you," I said.

"The pleasure is mine. What brings you in today?" She smiled at Cole. "Please tell me you aren't dating this guy."

I laughed. "No. We've been friends for a while now, and he's doing me a favor."

Cole explained why we were there and by the time he finished, Charlotte looked intrigued. "What day?"

"Wednesday if Daniel is available."

She winced. "Can't do Wednesday. I have a prior engagement. Did you ask Fletcher?"

Cole chewed his lip. "No, but that's a good idea. I'll see if she's free."

"Fletcher?" I asked.

"She's another reporter. New to town. Cole has asked her out three times and she flat out refused."

We grinned at each other. "Sounds like a smart lady."

"Hey!" Cole grumbled.

Charlotte snickered. "Make sure she meets Dakota and knows it's to help out a friend. Otherwise, she'll think you're being shady."

"I'm happy to talk to her," I offered.

"Who knows?" Charlotte said. "Maybe if you're on your best behavior, you can soften her up for a date."

Cole perked up at that.

"But don't be weird," Charlotte warned. "She'll smell fakery from a mile away." She turned her attention to me. "Fletcher is a better reporter than both of us. I think they'd make a good couple, but she's proven resistant to Cole's charms."

He held his hands up. "I stopped asking her out the second time she said no. There won't be a third time. She's going to have to ask me."

"Good luck," Charlotte said. "Dakota, I'd love to drop by the store sometime and check it out. I just transferred from North Carolina and still haven't been able to explore the town all the way yet."

"I just hired a new manager, but I pop in and out all the time." I fished through my purse and found a business card. "Take this and text or call when you want to come by, and I'll make sure I'm in."

She scanned the front. "Cool. Maybe next week?"

"Sounds like a plan."

Charlotte nodded. "Fletcher is in if you want to catch her."

He let out an aggrieved groan. "You better have something amazing planned on Wednesday," Cole grumbled.

Her eyes lit up. "Oh, I do."

We waved goodbye. Cole dragged his feet on the way to Fletcher's office.

I elbowed him. "Got it bad for her, huh?"

He snorted. "Used to. Now she's a pain in the rear."

"The best of us are."

Cole rolled his eyes and stopped at an office a few doors down from Charlotte's. He knocked and poked his head in. "Fletcher? You got a minute?"

A deeper feminine voice with a slight accent responded. "Come on in."

I followed behind him and stopped in my tracks. Fletcher was stunning. Flame-red hair, bright green eyes, heart-shaped face...I understood why Cole was smitten. Her face brightened when she saw me.

"I know you! I've been in your shop. We haven't officially met, but I've met your assistant."

"Oh!" I would have definitely remembered meeting this woman if she'd stopped in, so I must have been out. "Harper was just promoted to manager."

Fletcher nodded. "I thought she was wonderful." She stood and came out from behind her desk. The woman was tall and curvy. She was dressed more casually than any of us but wore a soft green blazer to keep it business-like. A pair of dark-wash, cropped flare pants, a white t-shirt, and mustard yellow flats gave her a professional yet creative flare. She stuck her hand out. "I'm Fletcher O'Day."

We shook. "Dakota Adair."

"Pleasure." Her gaze flicked to Cole. "What are you doing with this guy?"

Cole sighed which made me laugh. "We're here to ask you a favor, actually," he grumbled.

"Oh?" Her eyes narrowed.

I put Cole out of his misery and took over. "Yes. Cole and I are friends, and I asked for his help with an investigation of sorts. I haven't officially announced this, but I expanded Tattered Pages and formed a P.I. Firm. A friend of mine asked for some help with a potential stalker case, and Cole suggested one of the reasons might be due to jealousy."

Her eyebrows lifted. "The stalker is female?"

"We aren't sure yet, but I'm leaning that way. My plan is to ask Daniel out and pretend it's a date. Cole will be there doing surveillance and thought it best to have a female companion with him to make it appear innocent."

Fletcher's lips curved up. "Is that right?"

I snorted. "We asked Charlotte first, but she's unavailable on Wednesday."

She crossed her arms over her chest and studied us. "This isn't some roundabout way to get me to go out with you, is it?"

I pressed my lips together as Cole threw up his hands. "I knew you'd think that!"

"It's not," I said, a chuckle escaping before I could stop it. "Unless he has some mastermind strategy. If you aren't comfortable with this, we can always find someone else. Charlotte is the one who suggested it."

She studied Cole, her eyes narrowing. Cole stood still as a statue.

"Wednesday? Where?"

Cole looked at me.

"I'm not too sure yet. Everything is up in the air until I speak with Daniel. If you want to give me your number, I can call you once I know."

Fletcher leaned over and grabbed a card from her desk. "I'm free that evening." She glanced at Cole. "If we do this, you pay for the drinks and the meal."

Cole answered far too quickly. "Okay."

"And I will meet you there and leave as soon as it's over. Don't ask me to go anywhere else or do anything afterward."

"Okay," he said again.

I studied Cole for a long moment. There was an intensity in his gaze that gave me pause.

"Fletcher? How long have you been working here?"

She squinted. "Maybe six months or so?"

"Ah." That was around the time Cole started going through women like the daily newspaper. I suspected my friend was head over heels for an unattainable woman. "Well, welcome to Silverwood Hollow."

"Thank you. Give me a call once you know the details." She held up a finger and pointed at Cole. "No funny business."

He held up his hands like he was getting mugged.

"Absolutely none. We don't even have to talk if you don't want to."

Fletcher snorted. "We have to make it look natural. Otherwise, this will go south as soon as it starts."

"I really appreciate this." Waving the business card, I headed to the door. "We hope it won't be more than a couple of hours until we get some needed intel to move forward. As a side note, this is completely off the record."

Fletcher smiled. "I assumed. I'm always happy to help a woman in need." She winked and shooed us out.

Cole sagged as soon as we turned the corner.

"You're in love with her, aren't you?" I whispered.

He groaned. "It's so stupid."

"Love is never stupid," I responded. "But if she's not interested, you can't do anything to change it."

He shook his head. "I'm aware, but I can't help but think there's a spark there." Cole ran a hand through his blond hair. "I've been very good about respecting her space, but this date might kill me."

I stopped in my tracks. "First, it's not a date. Going into this thing thinking it is will place unrealistic expectations on both of you. It's work."

"You're right," he murmured.

"Second, promise me you won't push her boundaries."

"I would never do that."

"If you don't want to do this, we don't have to. There's bound to be someone else we can ask." I grinned. "I think Mom is free."

Cole laughed, the strain on his face easing. "I'll be fine.

If it gets to the point where I need to bow out, I'll let you know."

"Sounds good. I'll call Daniel this evening and get everything set up."

We said our goodbyes and hugged each other at the door.

Fletcher stayed on my mind for quite a while that day. Cole was a good catch, but the heart wanted what the heart wanted.

Maybe that just wasn't him.

SEVEN

"A date?" Daniel sounded dumbfounded.

"A pretend date," I clarified. "If jealousy is the reason behind this, it might draw out your stalker."

"Hmm. That's a good idea. Pretend, though?"

"Yes," I said patiently. "I'm still not ready to date anyone."

"Can we *pretend* it's not a pretend date?"

I laughed. "Daniel. We have to pretend it's a real date, but we also have to stay aware of our surroundings. Cole will be there watching, too, just in case we miss something. He invited a fellow reporter to go with him to make it look real. All off the record."

"I knew you were the right person to ask. Alright then. What day?"

"Wednesday evening. You name the place. I don't get out too much."

"Rocco's. Wear something nice, but not too flashy. I'll pick you up."

"Done. I'll let Fletcher and Cole know."

"Make sure you come hungry. Their food is divine."

"I'll keep that in mind. Take care."

"See you soon, Dakota."

After we hung up, I took my notebook out and made some notes.

Alice was next on my list. I'd forgotten to ask Cole about her, so I texted him.

He responded almost right away and said he didn't know her, but he'd see what he could find in the morning.

I had a thought, so I texted Daniel to ask if there were any authors he considered competition and if he'd ever had any run-ins with them.

His text back said he didn't consider any of them competition because there was enough to go around, but there was a fellow crime writer who messaged him a few times about similarities in their work. The problem was that Daniel had always turned his work in first.

He shot me over the name when I asked, and I added it to the bottom of the list.

I skimmed my notes and groaned. It felt like all I had was suspects and no leads. Who knew if the person would even know about our date?

We need to ensure we update our social media the night we go out, I texted.

A picture? With both of us? In fancy clothes? Ooh. Are

you going to tell Hardy in advance, so he won't get the wrong idea?

I let out a heavy sigh. *No. He's dating again. We've put boundaries in our relationship, so there's no reason to let him know beforehand.*

Daniel's reply took a while to come through. Those three little dots stopped and started. *I see*, was all it said.

Then, *I'm sorry.*

Nothing to be sorry about. I knew it would happen eventually.

Are you okay?

Not really, but I answered, *I'm fine.*

Wear a dress.

I rolled my eyes. *Maybe.*

Please.

Go to bed, Daniel.

I set my phone aside and crawled into bed smiling.

THE NEXT MORNING, I didn't go into the store right away. Instead, I lounged at home and enjoyed my coffee before checking my email to ensure Harper had sent me the signed offer letter back. Once I'd confirmed, I worked on adjusting the payroll to ensure her raise showed up during the next pay period.

Poppy jumped up while I was working and curled up in my lap, a rare enough occurrence that it made me pause, but I gave her a few scratches and let her be. Maybe she needed some lounge time, too.

When that was finished, I perused the notes about Daniel's case again and was just about to start researching his publisher when my phone dinged with a text.

Cole's message was short and to the point.

Call me.

Concerned, I did just that.

"Dakota, are you sure this is the right name?" His voice sounded odd, shaken almost.

"Yes. I got it from Daniel."

"If this is Alice Merritt, *the* Alice Merritt, I think you should stop looking into her."

I didn't understand. "What's so special about Alice Merritt?"

Cole's bark of laughter got under my skin. "Cole! I'm not going to drop it just because you tell me to. Who is she? I looked her social media up and didn't see anything."

"Her social media doesn't announce anything. She's the socialite daughter of the head of a newspaper conglomerate."

I waited and when he didn't respond, I said, "Okay…"

"It means if she's responsible for this, I think you're in way over your head, and you should back off before it gets dangerous."

A frustrated sigh escaped me. "Cole, I still don't get it. Why in the world would I be concerned about that?"

"It's not you, necessarily. If it's Alice, she might be trying to bring Daniel down in fantastic fashion. And she might get away with it."

I clicked my tongue. "I think not. If it's her and I can expose her, don't you think I should?"

"It's not what I think or don't think, but money makes the world go round. I'll go with you to dinner, but if there's any evidence that it's Alice, I'm going to bow out. Her father controls most of the newspapers in North America, and journalism is the only skill I have. I'll be persona non grata if I get caught up in this and he finds out. Don't make me become a barista."

"The town is in need of a good coffee maker," I said lightly. "You sound kind of paranoid, though."

"Dakota." His tone turned grave. "You should be worried too. Don't you receive new releases from publishers all the time? You have a good relationship with them?"

"I do. Why?"

"Because he could change that if he really wanted to."

My jaw dropped. I sat back against the couch cushions, my thoughts racing. "I need to call Daniel."

"Yes," Cole said. "That's a good idea, I think."

"Let's keep Wednesday scheduled. There's a good possibility nothing will happen, but if it does, maybe we can rule her out before it goes too far."

"Okay then. Be careful."

We hung up, and I got up to get another cup of coffee.

What had Daniel Jensen gotten me into?

I called Daniel on the way to the shop, but it went straight to voicemail. Not too common, but I knew he was getting ready for the upcoming release, so I left him a voicemail to call me back when he had a chance.

Poppy lay in her hammock, batting at an imaginary speck with her paw. I thought about tying a toy to the top of it for a while now but kept forgetting to buy one every time I went into the pet store. She seemed content without it, but I'd recently discovered she really loved toys, especially ones that wiggled and bounced.

It was for my entertainment as much as it was hers.

"Alright, grumpy," I said once I'd pulled in the spot in front of the store. "It's time to get out." She let me carry her inside before wiggling out of my arms and bounding across the shop, much to the delight of several customers who saw her.

The sound of her bell jingling as she ran made me chuckle.

Harper grinned when she spotted me. I waved and slipped to the back so as not to bother her. Once I'd set everything down and took a few minutes to skim over the reports, I went back out and started up the second register.

Harper and I worked together for a while until we'd cleared all the customers out. When the last one had gone, Harper slumped against the register.

"Whoa. That was an early rush!"

I grinned. "Maybe they're all here to see the new manager."

Harper laughed. "Hardly. I've been a fixture here since you opened. There's nothing much to see here."

"You never know. With great power and all that."

She snorted. "What brings you in today?"

"I wanted to show you how I order new releases and pick new books to stock. Do you have a little time?"

Her eyes lit up as she rubbed her hands together. "Oooh. You're teaching me how to buy books? I have all the time in the world."

"Great. Come on back then."

As Harper followed me to the office, I couldn't help but think I should have done this a while ago.

EIGHT

It was the day of my not date. I wore a mid-length, A-line black dress with a skirt that flared out and swirled when I moved, paired with matching kitten heels. I'd put my hair up in a messy bun, leaving a few stray curls loose, and added a pair of garnet earrings with a matching necklace. Fancy makeup application had always been beyond me, so I did what I always did when I had to wear it. A little tinted CC cream, winged eyeliner, pink blush, and a soft berry lip stain.

Daniel's vehicle pulled into the drive. I gave myself one last look and grabbed my wrap and purse on the way out the door. We decided to take the picture as soon as we got to the restaurant and put the location there. Risky but necessary.

If Hardy and I were on better terms, I would have asked him to watch our back, but I couldn't always rely on him to be there. Not anymore.

It was better off this way.

Daniel stepped out of the still-running vehicle, his eyes grazing my skin. He said nothing for a long moment before clearing his throat and coming around to the passenger door to open it for me.

"You look stunning," he murmured.

I'm glad it was dark because I blushed from the top of my head to the bottom of my feet. "Thank you. You clean up nicely."

He did. He wore a nice suit with a maroon tie. There was no way he could have known what jewelry I was wearing, but it looked like a deliberate choice. We matched in an odd way.

I slid into his vehicle and soon enough, we were on our way.

Rocco's didn't allow any vehicles in their parking lot, so Daniel turned his keys over to a valet.

"You ready?" he asked quietly.

My heart felt like it was pounding out of my chest. "Too late for doubt," I said.

He chuckled and extended his hand to help me up the stairs. As soon as my hand slid into his, I wondered if I'd made a mistake. Here was a handsome, successful man who'd made no secret about his interest in me, and I was taking him on a fake date.

Ugh. How did I get myself into these situations?

A well-dressed hostess led us to a table against the wall, next to a large window overlooking a small man-made lake.

Cole and Fletcher should already be seated. Daniel had used his pull with the management to get us seated in the best area that would allow someone to easily spy on us, but also to let Cole spot that person.

The weather called for rain later this evening, so the outdoor area was shut down, which worked in our favor. Several open tables were scattered around us. I caught sight of Cole but didn't acknowledge him other than a look. He gave a slight dip of his head, but other than that, his attention was solely on Fletcher.

I wondered if that was a mistake. If he were with Charlotte, would he pay more attention?

Now was not the time to doubt Cole, I admonished myself.

Daniel held my chair out. I smiled up at him and sat down, adjusting my skirts around me. He handed the camera to the hostess and asked for a quick shot.

When it was done, Daniel handed over the phone for my approval. It was a great picture of us, although I looked a little bewildered.

I laughed and nodded. Daniel grinned and thanked the hostess, who nodded and walked away.

"You're going to have to at least look like you enjoy spending time with me," Daniel murmured, his eyes twinkling with amusement.

"I do!" I hissed. "It's nerves."

"Mmm. Cole looks quite taken with the woman he's with. You sure that's not a real date?"

I groaned. "I was just thinking about that. She's turned him down several times, and she was the only one available to come tonight."

"That's the look of a smitten man," Daniel observed, shaking his head.

I pulled the wine list to me like a lifeline. "Let's hope he doesn't only have eyes for her tonight."

"If he does, it won't be a bad thing for me. We are in public, dressed up, and out to dinner together." He gave me a devilish smile. "Even if it's a pretend date, I can pretend it's real. At least for a little while."

I glanced up at him in surprise, my heart melting at his words. "Daniel?"

"Hmm?"

"You can have any woman you want. Why are you pursuing me?"

He blinked in surprise before letting out a deep, rumbling laugh. The sound of it shocked me, making me laugh along with him. It was a beautiful, free laugh. I'd never heard it before.

I liked it. A lot.

Daniel and I laughed together all the time, but this was something different. A little surprise, a little wonder, and a lot of amusement all rolled into one.

When he stopped, he wiped his eyes. "Are you serious?"

Was this a trick question? "I-yes. Why wouldn't I be?"

His smile softened. "Because it makes me even more determined to win your heart."

My hands stilled before I could turn the page on the menu. "What? Why?"

"You think so highly of me, but not of yourself. I hope to change that. You can't see what makes you so amazing. We've been friends for a while now, and I've never once felt like you were with me for any reason other than that you wanted to be."

"I would never treat a friend like that."

"I know. You do things for me and call just to talk. You rarely ask me for anything, and if you do, it's never actually for you. It's to help someone else."

I closed the menu, my blood rushing through my veins. "Daniel—"

"You are beautiful, dark-haired and blue-eyed. Your smile fills my day with joy. Not seeing you feels like the worst thing that could happen to me. I do not agree I could have anyone I wanted simply because they would want me for the wrong reasons. If you ever wanted me, I know it would be for the right ones."

My cheeks heated.

"I have made my interest known, but never in a forceful way. You've had your share of heartache to deal with, and I've always respected your space. I am your friend, Dakota, and I always will be, but I hope that you will allow me to be more."

My chest felt tight. Tears swam in my eyes.

"Sometimes you meet people you know will irrevocably change your life. You'd know their scent or the feel of them in a dark room no matter where you were. The words they speak are always important, and spending time with them never feels like a chore, only a privilege. You are that person to me. I knew my life would change the moment I met you, and only time would tell if it was for the better or the worse." He reached over the table and took my hand.

I swallowed hard, my dry throat clicking. No one had ever spoken such poetry—made me feel beautiful and wanted in only a few sentences. And the way he looked at me...

"I want you to choose me, Dakota. I want to spend every single day proving to you that the only woman I want is you."

Goodness gracious, sakes alive.

"You didn't wait long, did you?" A familiar voice said from above.

I jerked in surprise, pulling my hand away from Daniel's.

Hardy stood above us, dark brows pulled together. "Is this official now?"

My mouth fell open. "That's unfair," I croaked. "We're on—"

"A date." Daniel rose.

Someone from across the room swore. I turned, only to see Cole staring at a space somewhere behind Hardy.

"You've moved on, it seems," Daniel said. "Dakota has chosen to as well."

Hardy's jaw tightened.

"Who's your lovely date?" Daniel asked.

Hardy's look would have turned him into ash if possible. He took a step to the side, revealing someone I already knew.

Charlotte.

A strangled laugh broke from me as we stared at each other in shock. "Hello," I wheezed.

"Dakota." Charlotte's brow wrinkled as she looked from me to Hardy. "I take it you know each other?"

"You know her?" Hardy demanded.

Charlotte gave him a dark look. "Yes. First of all, it's a small town."

"Which is why I took us to a restaurant outside of that small town," Hardy growled.

Daniel's eyes danced.

I wished the floor would open up and swallow me whole.

When I caught Charlotte's eyes, I gave her the tiniest of head shakes, hoping she would understand what I was trying to tell her. She couldn't tell Hardy this wasn't what it looked like. Too many prying eyes rested on us now.

She inclined her head. "She came by the office the other day to meet with Cole. I popped into his office, and he introduced her."

Charlotte was good people.

Thank you, I mouthed.

Hardy turned to me, and it was like a light switch turned on inside his thick skull, and he realized how ridiculous he was being. "I—my apologies for the rude interruption."

One of Daniel's eyebrows rose. He stuck his hand out.

"Daniel Jensen," he said to Charlotte. With a wicked grin, he added, "Dakota's date for this evening."

Charlotte snorted. "Yes. I can see that." She jerked a thumb at Hardy. "This is our first date." There was a long pause. "And probably our last, too."

Hardy winced.

"I'm sorry," I said quietly. "Please don't take it out on him. It's just..."

"Complicated," Hardy said. "I overstepped a boundary here. Both of you, please accept my apologies."

Daniel and I both nodded.

"If you'd like to try, I hope to salvage this date," he said to Charlotte. "And hopefully make amends for my appalling behavior."

Charlotte gave him a long look. "You're buying dessert."

His shoulders lowered in relief. "A dessert tower. A truckload of it. Whatever. It's yours."

Charlotte winked at me and took Hardy's arm. "Then let's go. I hope they have tiramisu."

I buried my face in my hands. "Of all the people to run into tonight."

Daniel laughed. "I like Charlotte. Gracious and witty. Perhaps they'd make a good match."

"Maybe they would," I murmured, surprisingly not that upset about it. Charlotte seemed wonderful.

He reached for my hand again. "Think about it."

I nodded but was lost for words.

"Wonderful. Let's look at the menu, then. The pasta here is divine."

After we'd stuffed our faces with food and wine, Cole meandered by our table and snagged an extra seat.

"Fletcher went home. We saw no sign of Alice, but there's something you should see."

I sagged in relief. "Someone was watching us?"

"Yes, but there's more." Cole punched a few things on his phone screen before placing it face up on the table and pressing play on a video.

A couple sat closer to the middle, angled in a way where I wouldn't have noticed them unless I turned around. I didn't recognize either one.

"They're recording us?" Daniel asked, confusion evident in his voice. His brow furrowed. "Why?"

Cole shook his head. "I think someone hired a P.I. to keep an eye on you."

I laughed in disbelief. "What in the world have you gotten yourself into?"

"I've never been married. I have no children. My criminal record is spotless." His sigh sounded heavy. "I genuinely have no idea why someone would hire a professional to follow me around."

"At a minimum, we know someone is stalking your social media. The first thing you should do is clean up your friends list. You posted it on your personal account?"

"Of course. Too dangerous for the public account."

Cole interjected. "I'd check and see if someone has

their location turned on and see if they were in this area. Could narrow some culprits down."

"I don't think this is about me," I mused. "They're far more interested in Daniel, I think. There's no one on my social media I don't know. Except for the bookstore page, but I don't post anything personal there. Only business."

"We still can't rule it out," Cole cautioned. "Do you know where Alice is now?"

Daniel shrugged. "I haven't spoken to her since the breakup. She lives in the state, but I'm not sure where she is now."

"You know who she is, don't you?" Cole asked.

Daniel tilted his head in curiosity. "I'm not sure I understand the question. Of course, I know who Alice is."

"The socialite part?"

Daniel's eyes narrowed. "Excuse me?"

"Lord, love a duck," Cole muttered. "Do neither of you follow the social pages? How long did you date her for?"

"Six months." Daniel's cheeks turned pink.

Cole let out an incredulous laugh. He pulled up the search engine on his phone and typed something in. Daniel went pale as he skimmed down the page.

"I—" He rubbed a hand over his face. "In my defense, I was very heavy into deadlines at the time. Alice was a distraction, and I confess I never gave it much thought. We met at a signing, and I thought she was a pretty and intelligent woman. That's all."

I chewed on the inside of my cheek. "This wouldn't fit the socialite profile, would it?"

Cole turned an amused look at me. "And what profile would that be?"

I squirmed in my seat. "Don't they go through men like candy? Always on someone else's arm and onto the next as soon as the current one fizzles out?" Reality television and social media weren't on my favorite list, but I'd read my fair share of news articles in the gossipy magazines I got in the mail.

Cole's expression turned thoughtful. "I have a friend who works at a major newspaper in Nashville. Let me call him and see if he has any intel."

His prior words came back to me. "Be careful. I don't want you to get into any trouble over helping me."

"He's trustworthy," Cole assured me. "Ruling her out would be a huge relief."

Daniel stuck his hand out. "Thanks for your assistance and discretion."

They shook. "Anything to help Dakota." Cole straightened and tucked his phone back into his pocket.

"How'd it go with Fletcher?"

He gave me an amused look. "None of your business, that's how." Cole winked and turned away, shoving his hands in his pockets on the way out.

Daniel laughed. "Sounds like it might have gone okay."

"He'd be in a worse mood if it hadn't," I remarked.

"Dessert?" Daniel asked, flipping open the small menu a server had discreetly dropped by earlier.

I patted my stomach. "If you have something, I'll have a bite. Otherwise, no thank you."

He perused the menu. "I may order a little something just to drag this thing out. If I can't take you on a real one, I'm going to make this last as long as I can."

My cheeks heated. What was I doing? He was handsome, talented, smart, and he liked me. A lot.

I kept pushing him away out of fear. He was everything Hardy was not. There were times I thought Hardy would never accept me for who I really was. We'd fought about it multiple times. Maybe everything that happened did so for a reason.

I couldn't deny I felt an attraction to Daniel. Maybe it was time I did something about it. Hardy obviously had.

Daniel lifted his head and blinked. "What? Do I have something on my face?" He scrubbed a hand over his mouth. "Why are you looking at me like that?"

I opened my mouth, then snapped it shut. "No reason."

"Dakota," he growled.

I dropped my eyes. "I'm sorry," I said. "I've been a fool."

Daniel said nothing for a long moment. "I'm not sure what you're apologizing for. You've done nothing wrong."

I lifted my face, meeting his eyes. The understanding in them sent my blood racing. "When this is over, we should talk."

"Oh?" The words were steady but fraught with meaning.

I nodded.

His eyes flashed. "Over dinner?"

"Not in public."

His brows lifted. "Over chess?"

I slowly shook my head. "At my house."

"Oh." His breath whooshed out seconds before a brilliant smile lit his entire face up. "Absolutely."

NINE

I was at the bookstore bright and early the following day, waiting for Harper to show up. Poppy sat on the desk close to the register, watching the door with eerie chartreuse eyes. She never interacted much with Harper, but she wasn't antagonistic either. This was high praise on Poppy's part.

The bell jingled. Poppy meowed as Harper came in, holding a drink tray with two steaming coffees inside. I hurried over to help her, holding the door as she wrangled all her stuff in.

"Whoo!" she breathed, smiling at me as she set her stuff down on the desk. "It's getting chilly out there! I can't wait for all the festivals to kick off."

She scratched Poppy behind the ear and unwrapped her scarf from her neck. "You're here bright and early." Harper gave me an odd look. "Everything okay?"

"All good. I wanted to show you a few more things

before I took off for the day, and we needed to go through a few applications. Did you set up an interview for the girl you were interested in hiring?"

"Next week," Harper said, handing me over a coffee. "Salted caramel hot chocolate," she said. "They hired a new barista."

I gasped as I took it. "Oh, please don't let me down," I begged.

Harper laughed. "I haven't tried mine either, but the place was hopping with customers, so I have high hopes."

I pulled the stopper from the slot on the lid and took a cautious sip. Flavor exploded in my mouth. The bite of the salt, the sweetness of the caramel, the slight bitterness of the chocolate.

"Oh my," I moaned.

Harper took a sip. Her eyes fluttered shut. "Wow. I guess we were right. The new barista is a hit."

"It happened so fast. They must have been planning it for a while."

"Yeah. They should have started with her. The shop has probably already lost some customers due to the rocky opening."

"I wonder if they'll do any baked goods."

I could only imagine how successful they would be if they brought in a good baker. "If they have chocolate chip scones, I'm going to die."

We saluted each other with our cups. "Want to head back and go through some things before we open?"

"Lead the way, boss."

· · ·

MY CELL RANG JUST as I was wolfing down a burger in my car. I was on my way to the library to do some research into Daniel's publishing company.

"Hey Daniel."

"I got another call," he said. "This one doubled the amount. They claimed to have proof."

I winced, realizing I hadn't told him about the packet I received. I couldn't believe I almost forgot about it. "What kind of proof?"

I chewed on my lip as my mind raced. Should I tell him or keep investigating to figure this out? I didn't think he was guilty, but there was no way to be a hundred percent sure until I got to the bottom of the case.

"They didn't say." His heavy sigh came over the line. "I rarely worry about anything, but this feels like it might be something. Even though I know I didn't do anything!" Daniel groaned. "I feel like I'm being held hostage over something I had nothing to do with."

His words rang sincere.

"I'll figure this out. I promise."

"I know. I just..." He blew out a breath. "I want you to know I didn't do what they're accusing me of."

"I know," I said softly, and as I said it, I realized I truly believed it. Daniel didn't need to know about those papers for now. I'd tell him once everything was over.

"I have a call with my agent later this afternoon. I'm thinking about telling her what's going on."

"Wait," I said. "Just for a little while longer. Next week, we can sign the contract, and I'll have more leeway to investigate. Can you hold off that long?"

"My signing is in a little over two weeks. I have a little time. I'm working on my end, too. Hopefully, together, we can figure something out before it's too late."

He didn't sound all that hopeful. We said our goodbyes and hung up.

I had to get to the bottom of this sooner rather than later.

I rented a small little private office at the library, though *office* was too generous a word for what I stepped into. A box with a built-in desk, a PC, and a chair was more like it. I fired up the computer, smiling as the clicks and whirs of it sounded, and waited for the search engine to pop up. I'd purchased a subscription to a website, allowing me to do a deeper dive into publishers and agents, so I logged in and started researching Daniel's publisher.

An hour later, the only thing I found was an old Reddit post where someone complained about being rejected by one of their editors and mentioned something about their mentor during that project, not knowing excellent literature when they saw it.

I wondered if it was Daniel they were speaking about, so I took a picture of it on my cell and sent it to Daniel.

His response came almost immediately.

Yes! I almost forgot about that.

What happened?

He told me a story about being assigned to a few

people to mentor them on their writing projects, but said he dropped one individual almost immediately due to being a poor fit. The mentee didn't take it well.

I sighed. *Is this the same person in the critique group?*

No, he responded with a cry laughing emoji.

I slapped a hand over my face. *Maybe it's time to stop mentoring people? You might be bad at it.*

Daniel sent a shrug emoji back. *Maybe you're right.*

Back to square one. I went back to my research but didn't find too much more after that. Disgruntled, I packed up everything when I reached my two-hour rental limit and got back into my car to head home.

To my surprise, a vehicle sat in my driveway when I pulled in.

Hardy's vehicle.

I slid out of my car and headed up the steps to where he sat with his elbows on his knees, watching me.

"Hey," I said.

He rarely went unshaven, but Hardy had a five o'clock shadow and wore a haggard expression. "Hey. I'm sorry for showing up like this."

I had no idea why he was here, but I was glad to see him after everything that happened. "Don't worry about it. You're always welcome."

He let out a laugh of disbelief. "After the debacle at the restaurant?"

I tossed my purse by the door and sat down beside him. "We're all human, Hardy. I'm not going to throw away a relationship because of a single moment of anger."

He rubbed his face. "Why are you so good to me?"

It was my turn to laugh. "I don't think that's the case at all. I'm just understanding, I guess. I've done things I regret. We all have. I'm not going to walk away over it." I gently elbowed him. "Besides, we live in a small town. We're going to see each other all the time. The best we can do is try to get along, right?"

"Yeah," he croaked. "I'm here to apologize. Sincerely. I acted like an idiot."

"Just like I did the other day?" I asked lightly.

His huff of laughter made me smile.

"How's your daughter?"

His face lit up. "Good. She's adjusting really well to school and the new schedule."

"I'm glad. It's no easy thing to have your life completely upended."

"Which one of us are you talking about?"

"Both of you. Being a dad agrees with you."

He studied me for a while before he spoke. "But not with you."

"It isn't that. Not really. It's me. Not you. The thought of having children terrifies me. I was never sure I wanted any." I sighed and leaned against the porch post. "Eventually, it would have come up as a serious discussion, and it might have torn us apart."

Hardy's laugh sounded broken. "As I grew older, I was always on the fence, too. I leaned the same way you did about having children until one dropped into my lap."

"What a pair we are."

Hardy slung an arm around me. I scooted closer and leaned my head on his shoulder. "You had this entire other life I knew nothing about, Hardy. A fiancée. I've been a pretty open book, and there was a part of me that felt like I never got to know you. Not really."

"For what it's worth, I'm sorry for everything."

"You don't have to keep apologizing. You couldn't help what happened, but it wasn't the only thing that broke us up. We're both at fault."

When he chuckled this time, it sounded genuinely amused. "But I'm more at fault."

At my silence, his laugh deepened. "I accept that."

We sat there for several minutes, just listening to the night. "How'd the date go?"

Hardy snorted. "She let me pay for her dinner and dessert, then asked me not to call her again."

I winced. "You kind of deserved that."

"Yeah. I look at it as penance money."

We both laughed at that one. He gave me a quick squeeze and rose. "Are we good?"

I nodded. "We need to start treating each other as friends and not something more. It's the only way whatever this is will work."

He jogged down the steps and turned. "I agree." Hardy shoved his hands in his pockets. "Daniel is a good man, Dakota. I'm not saying I approve, because I'll never approve of anyone you date, but you could do a lot worse than him."

I studied him. "I'm not dating him, but I'm also not

saying it won't go that way. You ran a background check, didn't you?"

His eyes glittered. "I would never abuse my position like that."

He turned to go. "But I would assume someone like Daniel Jensen has a completely spotless record except for a speeding ticket two years ago that he took a deferment for."

"What a specific guess," I said lightly.

"Take care of yourself," Hardy said.

"Bye, Hardy."

This time, when the door shut, the goodbye felt final.

I stood, rubbing the chill from my arms, and let myself into the house.

TEN

I didn't get out of bed until nine the next morning. Harper was opening today, and I had nothing to do except get my fingerprints taken and take my polygraph.

After downing an embarrassing amount of coffee, I got dressed and headed to the address listed on my instructional email.

The fingerprinting place was two towns over, located in a squat, nondescript building with a small sign out front. The woman who helped me barked instructions, judging me when I accidentally smudged the first form.

By the time I left, I felt more humbled than I had in a long time.

Hopefully the polygraph went better. I headed all the way back to Silverwood Hollow and pulled into the police station parking lot. The procedure was in a different area from where Hardy worked, but after yesterday, I had high hopes things wouldn't be so difficult between us anymore.

As it was, I ran into him in the lobby.

He blinked. "Dakota?"

I waved and walked over to him. "I have an appointment to get a polygraph. Third floor, I think?"

"Want me to walk you up?" He held a coffee and a file labeled with a case number.

"If you have time, sure."

"Anything to get away from this case for a little while," he muttered.

When we were enclosed inside the elevator, he spoke again. "Is the test for your license?"

"Last step," I confirmed. "I just had my fingerprints done this morning."

He winced. "You saw Greta?"

I glanced up at him in surprise. "The mean one?"

Hardy snorted. "That's the one. She's like the overbearing, abusive mother I never had."

We both laughed. "She made me feel like I was about two feet tall."

"She's related to the owner and so close to retirement they've given up on firing her."

The elevator doors opened. He stepped out and waited for me. "It's down this way."

Hardy showed me to the glass doors and held them open for me. "I'll see you around. Good luck."

"Thanks for walking me up. Take care."

He smiled and walked away.

I let out a relieved sigh. The awkwardness was finally gone. It didn't mean it would be forever, but I had high hopes.

A woman behind the desk greeted me. After I signed in, I found a seat in the surprisingly busy lobby only to spot a familiar redhead.

"Fletcher?"

She looked up from her phone. "Dakota! I'm surprised to see you here."

"Last step for my license," I told her as I sat down next to her. "You?"

"Research for a story. I wanted to speak to someone about the nuts and bolts of it. Such a strange technology and still so important even though it can't be used in a court of law." Fletcher shook her head. "That never made sense to me. If it's required to achieve certain licenses and also for special agent jobs, why can't we use them in court?"

"Good point. I have no idea."

We smiled at each other. "Thanks for going with Cole the other night. I'm not sure what's going on with you two, but I appreciated it."

She shrugged. "My curiosity drives me to do many things I normally wouldn't."

I decided not to pry about Cole. It wasn't any of my concern, and I didn't want him to get upset with me for asking questions. "Well, you really helped me out."

"Did you figure it out?"

"Unfortunately not. We're working on it, though."

Fletcher's face grew thoughtful. "This is for your friend, Daniel?"

I nodded, but a wary feeling started growing in my stomach. "Why?"

"Do you think he would be amenable to a story about this?"

I shook my head. "You're welcome to ask him, but he was adamant everything be off the record."

"Drat," Fletcher muttered, but she didn't sound angry about it. "It's hard to dredge up good articles in a small town like this."

"You remind me of Cole. Must be in the reporter DNA."

Fletcher grinned. "We're all far too curious for our own good."

The double doors opened, and a woman poked her head out and called my name. "Gotta go." I rose and took my purse. "Nice seeing you again."

"How about lunch soon?" she asked. "It's difficult making friends when you're new in town."

I thought about it. As long as we didn't talk about Cole, I wouldn't mind having a female friend. "I'd like that. Text me?"

"You got it. I hope you're in the restaurant know." She frowned. "Maybe something that doesn't cost as much as that place the other night."

"That was an anomaly. I'd be broke if I ate like that every night." I waved goodbye and followed the woman to the back.

This was the last step until I was an official, by-the-book private investigator.

My stomach churned as I sat in the uncomfortable metal chair the woman directed me to.

Once I was hooked up, I closed my eyes and steadied my breathing.

Here goes nothing.

ELEVEN

I rewarded myself by getting a massive hot chocolate on the way home. As long as nothing out of the ordinary happened, or I failed my lie-detector test for some odd reason, I was home free. All I had to do now was wait for the results and send in the paperwork. Then I could officially open the doors and take new clients.

I took a detour toward Tattered Pages and stopped in to see Harper. To my surprise, Jane stood at the counter arguing with my new manager.

"I'm qualified, and you're hiring," Jane insisted.

My eyebrows rose. "Hi, Harper," I said, eyeing Jane as I went behind the register to stand beside her. "Everything okay?"

"Jane is interested in our opening." Harper's voice was level, but I could hear the underlying hint of anger.

"Oh?" I set my stuff down and tossed my empty cup into the trash can. "Did she fill out an application?"

"Not yet," Jane interrupted.

"Have you ever worked in a bookstore?" I asked.

"No, but I read all the time."

"Where are you currently employed?"

Jane's expression turned thunderous. "Why does that matter?"

"Because I call references before hiring anyone."

Jane deflected. "I'm the most qualified of anyone."

"How would you know that?" I asked lightly. "You don't even know who we're interviewing."

"I see the people coming in here!" Her face flushed.

"All the time?"

Harper shook her head and turned away.

"I—I'm downtown a lot." She snapped her mouth shut and glared.

Maybe I needed to keep a closer eye on her than I thought. "You're more than welcome to fill out an application. If we think you're a good fit for our opening, we will give you a call. Otherwise, we'll keep your application on file in case something else opens up."

Jane crossed her arms over her chest. "I feel like you aren't going to call me."

I smiled politely. "It depends on how you stack up against our other applicants."

Jane huffed and shoved her purchases across the desk. "Fine. I don't want these anymore." Harper caught them before they skidded off the edge.

The girl turned to go, but I cleared my throat. "Jane?"

"What?" she barked.

"You're walking on the edge of my patience right now. If you don't start showing some respect when you're in my shop, I will ban you from returning. Are we clear?"

Jane spun, her eyes wide. "You—you wouldn't!" she sputtered.

"I would. This is a private business, and I just promoted Harper to manager. She has full authority to ban you if I'm not here and you do something like this again."

Jane swallowed hard and looked down at her feet. "Sorry," she muttered.

"Have a good day, Jane."

She hurried out of the shop. Harper let out a long groan. "I'm sorry, Dakota. She's like a dog with a bone sometimes."

"Not your fault." I turned to face her. "What I said stands. If she does anything like that again, you're more than welcome to ban her from returning. We have far too many customers to put up with that nonsense."

Harper nodded. "Thank you."

"No need to thank me. I stopped in to see how things were going."

We both chuckled. "But I didn't plan to stay for long. Need anything while I'm here?"

"I have a book order ready to place. Mind giving it a once-over before you go?"

"Sure thing. Let's head back to the office."

. . .

LATER THAT EVENING, I sat on my couch sipping a glass of wine as I tried to figure out how to set up a new social media account. Alice had a public account, and I wanted to follow her without linking it back to Daniel.

I downloaded some stock photos and added those in of my supposed travels, along with some innocuous random shots from my cell phone camera that didn't show my face or any people.

Satisfied no one could link me to Daniel or my bookstore, I followed Alice, so I didn't have to remember to keep checking her account.

She added a new post while I was online of her in a bikini lounging on the deck of a massive boat. Or yacht, I suppose.

It didn't mean much. She could still be in town and posting pictures from earlier trips, but I kept it in the back of my mind.

Alice had way too much going for her to get this obsessed with Daniel. I couldn't account for people's mental state, and while I knew social media was a lie, Alice looked pretty happy in her photos. If she was off gallivanting in Greece, she couldn't be responsible for Daniel's troubles.

I pulled out the packet of papers someone dropped onto my porch and went through them again. Cole had dropped them back off at the store while I was out, requesting Harper not let them out of his sight until they were back in my hands. The pages revealed nothing new. I texted Daniel asking whether the phone call he received had the voice disguised.

He didn't text back for a few minutes, but he confirmed it had.

It wasn't a leap to assume the same person who called him had called my shop.

Want to eat dinner together?

I was on my couch in lounge clothes with wine. I got too comfortable. *You're going to need a winch to pull me off this couch.*

Want company?

If you're up for doing all the work, sure.

I'll be there in forty-five minutes.

No pasta! I'd had so much pasta lately, I might turn into a noodle.

No pasta, he agreed.

Daniel knew me well enough to know my favorites, so I trusted him to bring something I liked.

Be careful.

Always.

A little under an hour later, Daniel knocked on the door. I crawled off the couch with a groan and stretched before hurrying over to let him in.

He waved two bags of tacos at me.

"Ooh. I didn't know what I wanted when we texted, but you nailed it!"

I glanced back at the bottle of wine I'd opened. "I don't have any beer."

"I'm not picky. Red wine goes with steak, right?"

"I like your style, Jensen."

A few minutes later, we sat across from each other on the living room floor mauling tacos.

"I'm glad you came over tonight," I began.

His lip curved in amusement. "Oh yeah?"

"Because," I emphasized, "I think all the calls are from the same person. Mine didn't try to blackmail me, but they did want me to cancel your signing."

Daniel chewed, a thoughtful look on his face. "So they want money, and they want to ruin my career. I must have really ticked someone off."

"Do you know who *scribe1564* is?"

Daniel blinked. "How'd you get that name?"

I pushed the packet over to him. "Someone dropped this off on my porch."

He wiped his hands and flipped through the papers, the color draining from his face. "How did they get this?" Daniel rubbed a hand over his face. "Where—" His nostrils flared. "There's no way he had this. It's mine. I've never shared it with anyone except for my agent and editor."

"I asked the caller for proof, and this showed up at my door. I have to assume it's the scribe person."

"I never sent this to him." He rubbed his mouth. "None of my critique group ever saw my work. I only saw theirs."

"Who is this scribe person?" I asked gently. Poor Daniel.

"Ah." He shook his head as if to clear it. "His name is

Peter. I can't remember his last name. But he doesn't live in the state. He's somewhere in the Midwest."

"I can see what I find out about him. What group was it?"

Daniel's finger shook as he picked up his wine glass. "I'll have to text you later. I don't know the name off the top of my head."

"And you didn't get along in the group?"

"I wouldn't say that. Peter had issues with boundaries. I had to enforce mine, but that isn't a rare occurrence."

A furrow appeared between his brows. "How long have you had this?"

I grimaced. "A few days."

"And you just now brought it up?" His look speared me to the floor.

"Daniel—I—"

He slid his glass away and stood, gathering up the remains of his dinner. "You wanted to see if I was actually guilty." A heavy sigh lowered his shoulders. "After all this time, you didn't trust me?"

"It wasn't that." I stood up, wiping crumbs from my lap. "I wanted to give this more time to see if I could figure out who it was before I had to show you."

"And you wanted to make sure I hadn't done this."

I couldn't lie to him. "Every time I take on something new, I have to rule the victim out." My shoulders lifted in a shrug. "No matter how much I like the person, it wouldn't be a full investigation if I didn't."

Daniel's jaw tightened. "I see." He picked up his wine glass and trash and went into the kitchen.

"You can leave it," I said.

Daniel set the glass on the counter with a hard click, gathered his jacket and keys, and walked to the door.

"Please don't leave." I reached out for him. "You asked me to investigate, and that's what I'm doing."

"Consider yourself off the case."

My jaw dropped. "You can't be serious."

"I'm completely serious." He twisted the door handle and stepped onto the porch.

"You are being unfair," I accused, glaring at him from across the kitchen. "And egotistical. You know better than I do that I have to rule everyone and everything out."

Daniel's eyes flashed. "This is about trust, Dakota!" His voice snapped through the quiet.

I took a step back. "Yes, Daniel. It is."

We stared at each other. I had to resist the urge to scream at him over how idiotic I thought he was being. Of course I trusted him, but I had to dig deeper into his behavior to help me figure out why someone was targeting him. His career was on the line.

"If you want me to let this go, I will." I kept my voice level and calm. "But you don't have that much time before your signing and whoever it is has no plans to let this go. I have leads, and I think I'm close to figuring out who it is."

Daniel's nostrils flared. "I'll hire someone else. Send over your documentation via email. We haven't signed a contract, but I'll send over your retainer tomorrow morning."

"That isn't necessary." Tears welled in my eyes. "Daniel, please—"

He turned and walked away.

TWELVE

Sleep was elusive that night. I woke up the next morning feeling like I'd slept with my face in a sand pile. With a groan, I rolled out of bed and headed straight to the coffee pot, grateful for the scheduling feature.

Once I had a large mug of steaming java, I curled up into my reading chair and tried to think about the events of last night and where I'd gone so terribly wrong.

I thought about our argument all night long, but this morning surrounded by coffee and silence, my thoughts felt a little more balanced. I'd hit a nerve or something with Daniel. Whether it really was his belief that I didn't trust him, or something else was bothering him, something I hadn't figured out yet, I didn't know.

He'd always been so open with me, always willing to talk about things that bothered him, though I'd never been on that list. Not until now.

We weren't dating. He wasn't my boyfriend. But he was a friend. A good one.

And it hurt that he had walked away from me so easily.

My cell dinged with a text notification.

How about lunch today?

Fletcher. I could use some female companionship. There wasn't enough in my life. I responded and asked her how she felt about happy hour and appetizers.

It's my first love language.

I laughed out loud. Smiling, I made plans with her for five this evening. At least one thing about this day had started off right.

LATER THAT AFTERNOON, I scanned over the documents and sent everything to Daniel, along with a statement severing our agreement. It felt more like I was severing our relationship in more ways than one, but I shook that thought away and scolded myself for being over-dramatic.

Once that was done, I touched up my makeup and headed toward the best happy hour in town.

I'd discovered this place by accident a month or so ago when I popped in desperate for a quick bite and realized everything was half off from four to seven. It helped that the food was excellent.

Fletcher's flaming hair was like a beacon when I walked in. I made a quick left and navigated through the crowded tables. When she spotted me, her face lit up, and she waved.

"This place is great!" she said, her eyes wide as she took everything in. "I just sat down a minute ago, but I took the liberty of ordering us espresso martinis." She winced. "Too presumptive?"

I sat across from her. "Not at all. Thank you. Espresso martinis are one of my favorites."

"Then we have that in common." She pushed a menu over. "Anything you recommend?"

"I've only been here once, but the cheese curds are amazing. I also like the lettuce wraps and queso."

"All of those sound delicious." She skimmed the menu, tapping her fingers on the table.

We took a few minutes to decide and ordered as soon as the server came back over. When she walked away, Fletcher sighed.

"I'm so glad you agreed to meet me."

"Of course. I'm glad you asked."

The martinis arrived with the perfect amount of foam and three perfectly spaced espresso beans on top. There was an art to an espresso martini. I liked mine darker. Some liked them lighter. I felt like a true espresso martini left the cream liqueur out and only had the coffee, vodka, the coffee liqueur, and simple syrup.

This one was darker. I smiled and took a sip.

"This is perfect," Fletcher breathed. "Great idea, Dakota."

"I needed some drinks and apps after the last few days."

"New investigations are always difficult," Fletcher commiserated. "I'm on the other side of it, but there's the high at the beginning, the frustrating middle where nothing lines up, and then the part where it slowly starts to make sense, but you can't find that last piece to lock it all together." She took another sip. "Which part are you on?"

I plopped my elbow on the table and rested my chin on my hand. "The part where I get fired."

Fletcher's eyes widened. She set her martini down and winced. "Ouch. Can I ask what happened?"

I sighed. "I'm not really sure."

"We're still totally off the record," she reminded me. "Honestly, I'd much rather have a girlfriend than a story. So, tell me, please. If you want to. I'm all ears. And after another couple of these, I'm sure we will both be full of amazing ideas on how to solve all our problems."

I laughed. Fletcher had an easy way about her. She was beautiful but put on no airs. Slowly, I opened up about the case, leaving out most of the personal info and focusing only on the major things that led us to where we were.

She nodded sagely as I spoke. When I finished, she waved the server over and asked for another round. "Here's what I think." Fletcher held up a finger. "Men are prideful. They want to feel like they're the ones in charge. He's not in charge anymore, and when you held information back, it dinged his pride."

"I had to know for sure!"

She nodded. "I would too. My livelihood depends on not making mistakes. I'm sure yours does as well."

"I didn't do anything wrong."

"I never said you did. He feels like you don't trust him." Her eyes narrowed. "Were you two something..." She wiggled her fingers. "More?"

I studied her. Fletcher mimed zipping her lips. "Not yet," I admitted.

"But it was headed that way?"

"I think so."

"You wiped away his varnish, exposing his faults. He's probably not guilty, if everything you said is true, but his behavior might not have been perfectly gentlemanly. Maybe his ego got in the way. Maybe it was something else. He realized how deep you were digging and maybe it pricked something inside of him."

I sat back and thought about it. Her words made sense. But I didn't like them.

"His ego is more important than me?"

Fletcher held up a hand. "Whoa. No. I'm not saying that. Not exactly. My advice is to give it time. He seems to be an intelligent man, and the way he looks at you..." She shook her head. "He will apologize. If not, he's a gigantic fool."

Our appetizers came then. Fletcher and I dug in, silence falling for several minutes.

It gave me the opportunity to really think about her words and wonder what I wanted in life. People made mistakes; it was part of being human.

But I hadn't done anything wrong. I sat up a little straighter.

"Ah." Fletcher nodded. "I've seen that look before." She pushed a small bowl of ranch toward me. "Take it easy on him."

I snorted. "That's not really in my nature."

I HAD to hire a car to take me home. Four martinis later, I felt pretty good about the state of the world. I had enough caffeine in me to want to run a marathon, and sleep would be a long time coming, but it would give me the opportunity to go over Daniel's case one more time.

Yes, he had fired me, but he was my friend and deserved my help.

I no longer thought he deserved anything else from me, but I did care about him, and he had a book signing I'd dumped quite a bit of money into.

Daniel Jensen was getting my help whether he wanted it or not.

I paid the driver and headed inside, tossing my keys onto the hall table and missing by a mile. I'd pick them up tomorrow.

Kicking off my shoes, I headed straight for the bedroom and changed into a tank and soft pants, topping it with a cardigan and fuzzy socks.

I brushed my teeth and took my makeup off, then padded back into my living room and opened Daniel's file, spreading all the evidence across my kitchen table.

My gut told me Alice wasn't involved, or she wasn't the only one involved. I pushed all her stuff to the side. The scribe guy was my number one suspect, but Daniel's words from earlier gave me pause.

If Daniel wasn't guilty of plagiarism, how had they gathered this information? It had to be either his agent or his editor.

But that didn't make sense either.

Why would they release something like that when they were under contract with him? They had a symbiotic relationship. If Daniel made money, they made money.

It made no sense to jeopardize their reputation or their relationship with him. I didn't buy that angle.

I tapped my pencil on the table, my head still a little woozy from all the martinis. It might be better to examine this all tomorrow.

And drink water before bed.

Someone banging on the door startled me. I squeaked and dropped the pencil, almost falling out of my chair in my haste to answer it.

Tugging my cardigan shut, I hurried to the door and peeked through the peephole.

"Dakota!"

"Hardy?" I unlocked the bottom and the security chain and opened the door.

Hardy burst in, his arms wrapping around my waist. Startled, I flung my arms around his neck to hold on.

He swung me around, his face buried in my neck and

inhaled deeply. "Where have you been?" His voice sounded rough and ragged.

"I—I've been here." My heart pounded in my chest. "What's all this about?"

"I saw your car abandoned at a restaurant parking lot. No one remembered seeing you there. I tried to call you multiple times." He set me down. "Dakota. What in the world? Why isn't your car here?"

I unwrapped myself from him and blinked, surprise and confusion rushing through me. He'd rushed here when he thought something happened. He called multiple times. He'd come here for me. I licked my lips. "I went to happy hour with Fletcher, a new reporter who works with Cole."

He shut his eyes and exhaled, a huff of laughter shaking his shoulders.

"I had too many martinis and had to hire a car to take me home."

Hardy snorted and slapped a hand over his face, rubbing his eyes. "I thought something happened to you. I was so worried."

"Martinis happened," I said sheepishly.

His chuckles turned into a full belly laugh. Hardy leaned against the wall.

I let out a giggle, which soon turned into cracking up. Whether it was the martinis or the release of emotions after Hardy turned up...whatever it was, I needed it.

When the laughter died down, we stood there staring at each other.

"I'm sorry I worried you," I said quietly.

"I overreacted." He sighed and pushed away from the wall. "You've never once done that, and my thoughts immediately jumped to this case and..." Hardy shrugged. "My heart ran away before my head could catch up."

"Thank you for checking on me."

He took a step closer and reached for me. Hardy took me by the arms and bent to stare into my eyes. "I will always come for you."

Tears welled in my eyes. I reached up and stroked his cheek. "Hardy—"

He snagged me around the waist and pressed his lips against mine.

Hardy's touch felt like coming home.

THIRTEEN

I woke up confused and with a slight headache. Thank goodness I drank a ton of water before I went to bed last night.

After coffee and a quick breakfast of yogurt and granola, I showered and headed out the door. Before we parted ways, Fletcher offered to help with tracking down the scribe email address.

I usually went to Cole for this sort of thing, but it was kind of nice having a female friend. Or almost friend. We were firmly in acquaintance territory, but I had a good feeling about her.

I stopped at the new coffee shop and got us both lattes, then headed over to the newspaper. Fletcher spotted me and waved me into her office.

There was no sign of Cole, so I followed her in and offered her the other latte.

"Ooh. You know the way to a girl's heart." Fletcher

wore dark-wash skinny jeans, a white tank top, and a green cardigan with mustard-yellow flats. Her hair was tied up in a messy bun, and she wore a pair of tortoise-shell glasses. We both looked like two women who'd gone out for martinis the night before.

"Coffee. It's always coffee."

She grinned and popped the lid off, inhaling. "I had two cups already, but this morning I'm partial to three or four." Fletcher took a sip. "And maybe a greasy burger for lunch."

I shuddered. "Not sure I'd go that far."

She laughed. "Did you bring the email address?"

I pulled out the slip of paper and handed it to her. She skimmed it and went behind her desk, pulling out her keyboard tray. Her glasses slid down her nose, giving her a harried librarian look. Or the look of a woman who'd overindulged last night and barely had time to get ready for work.

I grinned at her. Fletcher snorted. "Don't tell my boss we went out last night. She's been trying to get me to go out for drinks for weeks now."

"You don't want to go?"

"With my boss?" She grimaced. "Absolutely not. Muddies the waters too much. I try to keep work strictly professional."

My eyebrows went up.

Fletcher shook her head. "Don't you dare say a word about Cole."

I mimed zipping my lips. "I would never."

"Sure you wouldn't," she murmured.

"Only if you hinted about it."

"I won't," she said primly. Fletcher fell silent as her fingers tapped across the keyboard. "This email address looks like a burner. I can't find the username anywhere, nor can I see where it's been used anywhere else."

"That's weird for a critique group, isn't it?"

Fletcher shrugged. "For most people, yes. Maybe there's a reason this person wants to keep their identity secret."

"Daniel said his name was Peter, and he was somewhere in the Midwest."

Fletcher slid the piece of paper across the desk. "That won't help the search. Have you tried emailing him?"

"I thought about that this morning."

"That's what I would do. See if he can meet you somewhere in the middle."

"In person?"

Fletcher laughed at the horror in my voice. "Or you can Facetime, but I find meeting in person gives you a better sense of people and their potential motives."

"I don't think he'll meet me in person, especially if he's blackmailing Daniel."

"You never know. There are a lot of dumb criminals out there."

I tucked the paper back into my purse. "Thanks. I'm not sure I've met any dumb ones yet. That'd be a refreshing change of pace."

Fletcher turned her chair around and faced me. "I'm happy to go with you if he agrees to a meeting."

"Thanks for the offer, but I doubt he'd agree to meet if I had a reporter in tow."

"I can sit in the car." She shrugged and stood. "Just keep it in mind. I'd hate for you to go alone and get into a situation where you needed help."

I stood and gathered my purse. "I'll let you know what he says."

Fletcher walked me out of her office. I spotted Cole. He stopped in mid-step, stared at us, and frowned.

"You didn't tell him we hung out?" Fletcher asked.

"I didn't see the need to."

A soft laugh escaped her. "I think we're going to be very good friends."

She tilted her head to Cole and escaped back into her office.

"What was that about?" he asked when I made a beeline for him.

"She's helping me out with something for Daniel."

"Oh?" Curiosity glimmered in his eyes. "Any reason you didn't ask me?"

"We chatted about it beforehand. No big deal. She couldn't help me, but I have a new plan going forward."

"If there's anything I can do, please ask."

"Of course." I reached up and gave him a quick hug. "Everything good?"

"All is well. You?"

"Same."

He laughed. "The same for you is way different from the rest of us. You lead an interesting life."

"No bodies. I'd say I'm already on the winning side."

He walked me out, stopping at the entrance to the door. "Take care of yourself. Call me if you need anything."

"Will do!" I waved and headed back to my vehicle.

I had an email to send.

To my shock, I had a response back within the hour. Peter, or whoever it was who owned the scribe email address, had no idea what I was talking about.

I gawked at the email. *Can we talk?* I responded back.

The next email was a phone number. I called right away.

"Hello?" The voice was young and male.

"My name is Dakota Adair. I'm calling over some concerning accusations about plagiarism."

Peter snorted. "Daniel Jensen. Right. I haven't heard from him in close to two months now. I was in an online critique group with him, and we didn't see eye to eye."

"Can you elaborate? Someone is trying to blackmail him, and he hired me to get to the bottom of it." I conveniently left out the fact that he fired me because it wasn't relevant to this conversation.

"Not much to elaborate on. He gave me some admittedly deserved critical feedback, and I reacted poorly."

The first step in becoming a better human was realizing you made mistakes.

"Did you ever tell him that?"

Peter sighed. "No. I believe Mr. Jensen blocked me after my second email. I tried, but I don't blame him for not wanting to speak to me again. It has to be difficult to be in his position. All I wanted was to succeed, but my ego was a little too big to learn anything until it was too late."

"It's never too late," I said.

"It is for him."

"Maybe so. I can pass this on to him if you'd like me to."

He paused. "Yes. I would. Thank you. Is there anything else I can help you with?"

"Did you drop a packet of papers on my front porch?"

A disbelieving snort came over the line. "I have no idea who you are, so I'm going to go with no on that one."

Then who had done it? A thought struck me. "My understanding is you live in the Midwest?"

"I do," he said slowly. "But I've only been here for a little while. I was in the process of moving while I was in that group."

My heartbeat picked up. "And where were you before the move?"

"A few towns away from the Silverwood Hollow area. The less touristy area."

"Interesting." I pulled my notebook over and scribbled down what I learned. "Can you give me a list of everyone who was in that group with you?"

I heard keyboard clicks. "I can do you one better. I have everyone's email addresses from the initial meet-and-greet message. Would that help?"

Finally, things were looking up! If I were thinking straight, I would have asked Daniel for it, but he only had concerns with one of his group members.

"That would be great. I appreciate it, Peter. Can you tell me anything about any of the other members? Any concerns or anything that stood out?"

"Not much. We had a Discord group for students only, but it was mostly people hashing out character and plot issues. I didn't participate too much."

He cut himself off. "This is probably nothing, but there were two girls who constantly gushed about Daniel. They were in some kind of competition to see if they could get him to go out on dates with them."

"Ah. That's helpful. Thank you."

"If I think of anything else, I'll call."

"I appreciate it. Take care of yourself."

"You too."

I sat back in my chair and tapped my pencil against my notebook. The news that he had lived around this area was curious. I didn't feel like he was lying to me, but I'd known him for all of five minutes. If he had no knowledge of what was happening to Daniel, then how did the person who dropped those papers off get a hold of them to use as evidence?

A thread I didn't like was starting to unfurl, and I was afraid if I tugged on it, everything would fall apart.

FOURTEEN

I sat at a cafe one town over, a place I'd never been before, flipping through my notebook as I tried to connect the dots. I hadn't heard from Daniel, but he also hadn't sent over the promised retainer. He wasn't the kind of man who forgot about much, so either he was angrier than I thought, or this was a quiet way to tell me to keep working.

Even if he had, I'd still continue working.

My cell dinged with a text.

How are you feeling?

I smiled down at the message. Hardy. *I'm okay. Thanks for asking.*

Are we okay?

I kept trying to put that incredible kiss out of my mind all day, but it was close to impossible. Fear could paralyze someone if they let it overtake them. Everything had happened all at once. The case I was working on overwhelmed us both. I still had doubts about whether Hardy would ever accept my work, and then his fiancée showed up with his little girl. All of those events could overwhelm even the most stalwart of hearts.

I backed away at first, then turned and ran.

But when he showed up last night, his first and only instinct to protect me, something inside of me thawed. I took a deep breath and sent the next message, knowing it had the potential to change everything.

How would you feel about introducing me to your daughter?

Officially.

The response took a while to come.

Are you sure?

I've never been more sure of anything in my entire life.

Yes. When?

In a couple of weeks. Let me finish up my current case. Whatever works for you as her parent. A public space, maybe? No pressure.

How about the zoo?

I laughed. *Maybe start with something a little less intense. A zoo visit takes hours. How about ice cream?*

No chain shops. Let's go to the artisan place.

Good with me.

I put my phone away just as the server arrived and dropped off my soup.

Baby steps. That was all I could do right now.

After I finished lunch, I called Fletcher to catch her up on my conversation with Peter.

"Totally clueless?" She sounded doubtful about Peter's

insistence he had no idea what I was talking about when it came to Daniel copying someone else's work.

"Yes. He sounds like he's telling the truth."

"Interesting. One of the most helpful things I learned in this job is when two things are too coincidental, they aren't a coincidence. If Peter was living here around the time of the critique group, and Daniel was, too, there's something you're missing. Something linking those two things together."

"I agree, but so far, I can't find the missing piece of the puzzle."

"It will come," Fletcher assured me. "It always does."

"Let's hope it comes soon. The signing is coming up very soon, and I'd hate for this to blow up in Daniel's face."

Fletcher clicked her tongue. "He hired you for a job. And then he fired you. You've done everything you were supposed to do."

"I know. But he's my friend. Even if he's mad at me right now."

Her sigh made me chuckle. "I hope everyone has a friend as good as you are, Dakota."

"Well, so far, I'm not doing a very good job helping this friend out," I muttered.

"You're doing much better than most people would be. You've ruled out Peter, linked the critique group and the link to your area and Daniel."

"Which doesn't tell me much," I interrupted.

"How many suspects do you have left?"

I skimmed my notes. "Three."

"Have you scanned any message boards about this?"

"No. It's a good idea, but he's very popular. I might not be able to figure out what's fact or fiction."

"If you see something unusual, look at their post history and follow it from there."

"Ugh. You've potentially added hundreds more suspects."

"I never said I would be a boring friend," Fletcher sang.

We made plans to meet up for lunch in a few days before disconnecting.

I pulled up to the house to see a familiar car in the driveway. This entire week felt like constant déjà vu.

Unlike Hardy, Daniel wasn't sitting on the porch. He leaned against his car, eyes covered by mirror sunglasses, and watched me pull in.

I got out, ensuring I'd tucked my notebook deep into my bag.

"Daniel," I greeted, my voice toneless. "Can I help you with something?"

"I'm here to apologize."

"You could have texted or called."

He shrugged. "I could have, but I didn't. You're still working on my case, aren't you?"

"If I am?"

Daniel smiled. "I wouldn't expect anything less from you." He crossed his arms over his chest. "When I thought you didn't trust me, it triggered something within me. I overreacted. I can't take it back, but I can do better."

"I accept your apology." I inclined my head and went to walk past him.

Daniel reached out and caught my arm. "But?"

I inhaled a long breath and let it out slowly as I turned to face him. "But I think whatever this is budding between us needs to stay on the ground."

"Dakota," he growled.

"I'm completely serious. You've known me for months now. We've worked together numerous times. I've always been there for you, and the one time I did something you didn't like, you lashed out and shut me out. You were willing to cut me off over something I saw as minimal." I snorted. "Not even minimal, honestly. Necessary. I was doing my due diligence on a case you hired me for."

To his credit, he didn't try to deny it. "You're right."

"It's a bad start to a relationship. When I tried to explain myself, you grew defensive and refused to listen to anything I said. That is a lousy indicator of future relationship success."

His jaw tightened. "You're right about that, too." Daniel pushed away from his vehicle. "What can I do to make this right?"

"Nothing. I've already accepted your apology."

"Friends or nothing?"

I gave him a short nod. "That's all I'm willing to give you. And we cut down our chess nights for a while."

"This sounds like you're breaking up with me on the friend front, too."

"I'm not, but just because I forgive you doesn't mean

I'm over it. I'm still mad at you. More hurt than mad, but I'm not ready to let everything go yet. I need some time."

He nodded. "I don't like it, but I'd rather have you as a friend than lose you. What about the case?"

"You fired me."

Daniel laughed. "And yet you refused to stay fired. Can I officially rehire you?"

I shrugged. "My rates have gone up."

"You're price gouging me now?" His eyes twinkled with amusement.

"Supply and demand, Daniel."

"Fine." He walked around to the driver's side of his vehicle. "Send me your rate sheet and contract. You should be official this week, correct?"

"I hope so."

"Alright." Daniel opened the door. "Remember, Dakota. Everyone deserves a second chance."

He might regret those words soon. I inclined my head. "I'll send you an email later."

"I look forward to it."

FIFTEEN

The internet was a savage no-man's-land, and I'd come entirely unprepared. Following Fletcher's advice to scour the message boards, I lay sprawled on the couch, surrounded by snacks and Reddit drama.

Daniel Jensen was the talk of the town—online, at least.

I knew an hour in, I probably wouldn't find anything usable here. Not long after that, I wondered if I'd dodged a sniper bullet by enforcing firm friendship boundaries and taking a big step back.

I gave Daniel the benefit of the doubt, but some stories here had me raising my eyebrows.

Two hours in, I was full of cheese puffs and despair at the human race. Just as I was about to shut things down, a random thread underneath the one I was viewing caught my eye.

Upcoming Signing. Has the wind changed directions?

I sat up straighter and clicked on the thread. The user was named *itgirl2000*, and it brought up accusations of plagiarism and Daniel finally getting his due.

For the most part, no one took it seriously. A few asked for proof, but most thought the person was a troll. I clicked on the profile, but it looked like a throwaway.

I screenshotted the thread, copied the username, opened a new window, and searched for it outside of the forums.

Again, nothing came up, but I wrote it down in my notebook. Once this was over, I should get something more official. Maybe something with my name on it. Engraving Clues on it might be a step too far. I snorted and stood, stretching out my stiff muscles.

My phone dinged a little while later. A quick check alerted me to a cash app payment from Daniel with a note that said *Adjusted Retainer*.

Smiling, I tucked my phone in my pocket and padded into the kitchen to rummage around for something to cook for dinner.

RAIN PELTED the yard early the next morning, fat drops of moisture and lower temperatures announcing the official arrival of autumn.

I stepped onto the porch with socked feet and a fuzzy cardigan, inhaling the fresh scent and smiling. My favorite time of the year. Cool, but not too cold. The smell of cinnamon and spices. Color-changing leaves and cider and all those wonderful, cozy sweaters. Mmmm. Yay, fall!

I'd woken up and decided to take a day off. A real one. Having Harper as my new manager made making decisions like this so much easier. I shot her a text confirming she'd be in and letting her know to text me if anything came up.

She shot me a thumbs up and a maple leaf.

Wrapping my hands around my steaming mug of coffee, I settled onto the rocking chair and listened to the rain for a little while.

Today was the first official fall market in the town square. The rain had thankfully cleared, leaving behind a cloudy, gloomy sky. I wrapped myself up in a tunic sweater, fleece leggings, and a warm scarf with a wool hat and headed over.

Even though the market was twenty minutes away from opening, a small crowd lingered around. Men, women, and children holding reusable shopping bags and baskets wandered the town square, peering in windows and oohing and aahing over the shop offerings. The market always brought in a little more business to my shop, but it wasn't overwhelming. Most people brought their kids the first week, and by the time they finished wandering the market, most parents were ready to take them home.

I sat in the car and waited for opening time, content to sip on a cup of coffee I'd brought in my travel mug. The radio droned, drowning out the sound of the crowd.

A quick glance around revealed a few things I needed

—apples, fresh ground spices, handmade pies, and a coffee bar I'd never seen before. The last two weren't technically needs, at least not on Maslow's pyramid. Just mine.

Even sitting in the car, the smell of fall infiltrated the cabin. This was Mom's favorite time of year, too. I hadn't seen her or Gran in a while, so I made a mental note to call them when I got home.

A woman with a reflective vest walked over and cut the ribbon to the market. A cheer went up around the square. I smiled and slid out of my vehicle, grabbing my basket and purse.

I waited until the bulk of the crowd entered before I followed behind. The scent of a familiar cologne tickled my nose seconds before a deep voice spoke in my ear.

"Come here often?"

A slow smile spread over my face when I recognized Hardy's voice.

"The first market of the season has the best apples for pie." I held up my basket.

"Plus, coffee, and pumpkins, and all the other wonderful things this place has?"

I shrugged. "That's why I brought a bigger basket."

Hardy chuckled. "Mind if I walk with you?"

"If you buy me a coffee." I winked at him.

"I knew there'd be a catch."

He looked good today. His badge was clipped to the waistband of dark-wash jeans, and he wore a dark-green pullover that made his eyes seem like they were glowing. His gaze swept the crowd, taking in anything suspicious or out of place. Silverwood Hollow might be safe, but there wasn't a single place on the planet without some danger.

He held up a finger and walked away, heading straight to the coffee booth. I smiled to myself and veered toward the apple vendor. He recognized me immediately.

"Miss Dakota!" He lifted a hand in greeting. "I knew I'd see you today." He was of indeterminate age, anywhere between sixty to eighty, with a heavily wrinkled face and bright, curious brown eyes.

"Hey, Martin. How's the apple crop?"

Martin leaned down and hauled up a massive bag of apples. "Better than usual."

My eyes widened. "Are those all for me?"

"If you want them. I have apples coming out of my ears."

"What's that bag...twenty pounds?"

"Give or take a few," he agreed.

How many pies could I make with that many apples?

Hardy came up beside me and handed me a cup of coffee. I smiled in thanks.

"Hello, Detective," Martin said. "I believe Miss Dakota is calculating all the recipes she could make with these." He swept a hand toward the bag.

Hardy blinked. "You're going to need a bigger basket."

"I want them all," I told Martin.

He beamed at me. "I thought you might."

I handed Hardy my basket.

He shook his head. "I'll carry the apples."

Martin laughed. "She can leave them here and pick them up on the way back, if that's agreeable."

"Very much so." We haggled a little on price, though I didn't argue too much because of his thoughtfulness, something he used to his full advantage. When the transaction was done, Hardy took the basket from me anyway.

"Where are we headed?" he asked.

"Spices next."

"Lead on."

I sipped the coffee and closed my eyes. He remembered the exact way I took it.

Hardy's eyes crinkled at the edges when he saw my look of surprise. "You're a difficult woman to forget."

Heat pinkened my cheeks, and I ducked my head.

We spent the next hour browsing the market when I saw someone who looked familiar and who shouldn't be here.

I frowned and tugged on Hardy's sleeve, signaling for him to follow as I navigated through the rapidly growing crowd.

A slim blonde woman browsed a stall across the market. I'd never seen her in person, but she constantly posted pictures on social media. And she was supposed to be in Greece.

"Who is that?" Hardy murmured, spotting the woman I fixated on.

"Alice Merritt," I whispered back. "She's on my list of suspects for Daniel's case."

His face briefly darkened at the mention of Daniel's

name, and I realized I hadn't filled him in on anything that had happened over the last few days. There was no reason to, but if things continued the way they might be, I would tell him.

A man stood beside her, his back turned to us. When he turned and I saw Alice tip her head up and smile at him, my breath caught.

It was Daniel.

What in the world?

Should I scratch her off my list? Or was Daniel doing his own investigation?

Hardy scowled.

"You don't have to come with me," I said quietly.

He didn't respond, but he stayed by my side.

Daniel's eyes widened when he saw me. His jaw clenched, but he pasted on a smile.

"Dakota." He spotted Hardy next to me. "Detective Cavanaugh."

Hardy coughed. Since when did Daniel call him Detective?

Alice had a guileless look about her. "Hello." Her voice was soft and breathy.

I stuck my hand out. "Nice to meet you. I'm an... acquaintance of Daniel's."

His eyes flashed with anger over that.

"And you are?" I probed.

"Oh!" she giggled. "I'm Alice. Daniel and I are dating."

A flash of hurt snapped through me. "Is that right?" My smile sharpened. "Is this new?"

"Not really, but sort of?" Alice giggled again. "We dated previously but broke up. Daniel called me yesterday, so I decided to drive down and see this market everyone keeps talking about!" She waved a pink cell phone at me. "I have to get some footage for my channel, and this is the perfect backdrop."

"Channel?" Bless Hardy's heart. He had no idea what an influencer was.

"Oh, yes!" Alice gushed. "I update twice a week, usually for my fans."

"Fans?" Hardy echoed.

I bit my bottom lip to keep from laughing.

"Are you coming to Daniel's signing then?" I asked.

Daniel's mouth opened, but Alice gasped. "A signing?" She tilted her face up to him. "I had no idea!" She looked back at me. "When?"

I rattled off the date. "You can follow the shop if you want updates." I gave her the social media handle. Alice's fingers flew over her phone keyboard as she tapped it in.

"Done! I'll be there."

I grinned. "Wonderful. It's always nice when the author's friends and family support them, isn't it?"

Daniel cleared his throat. "Dakota, may I speak with you for a moment?"

"Of course!" I made no effort to move.

Hardy coughed, covering up a laugh.

"In private?" Daniel took me by the elbow and hauled me over to the next booth.

"What are you doing?" he hissed.

"Nothing." Maybe needling him a bit, but that was all. "What are you doing?"

"I'm trying to figure out if she's the one responsible for blackmailing me!"

"By taking her to the market and making her think you're dating again? If she's not guilty of criminal behavior this go round, she might be if you're going to dump her again."

He blinked in surprise, his brow furrowing as if my words had triggered something.

"Did you not think about that?"

Daniel rubbed a hand over his face.

I burst out laughing. Men.

"Why didn't you wait for me to completely rule her out?"

He shrugged. "I don't know. You're mad at me, and you have responsibilities here, and I thought it was easier for me to figure out what she was up to than it would be for you!" He groaned. "Taking something off your plate was my obviously insane way of apologizing."

I put a hand on his arm. "Daniel. I'm not mad at you. I won't deny things between us have changed, but I'm still on your case as long as you want me to be, and I've almost ruled her out. There was no reason for Alice to come here."

"I didn't ask her to." He let out a breath. "I see you're with Hardy."

"He spotted me at the market," was all I would give him.

Daniel nodded. "I'm not mad."

"I should hope not," I blustered.

"I'm well aware I'm the idiot here." He snorted, which made me laugh.

Seconds later, we were both cracking up, a much-needed release of the tension between us.

Alice came over, a curious look on her face. "Everything okay?"

I turned. "Everything is perfect." Waving my coffee cup at her, I smiled. "I'll leave you two lovebirds alone. Hardy and I have a few more stops to make before I need to get home."

Daniel gave me an exasperated look. "See you around, Dakota."

I grinned and walked over to Hardy, curling my fingers around his arm.

He stilled, then smiled, and bent down to whisper in my ear. "Everything okay?"

"All good. Daniel thought he would help out with the case, and it appears to have backfired spectacularly."

Hardy grinned and led us away from them. "He's not dating Alice, is he?"

"Nope."

"I could tell when a look of horror crossed his face when she said it."

We both laughed. "Not my circus," I said at last.

"Good. How about we go check out the pie booth?"

"You always know the right thing to say."

Hardy tugged me closer. "Pie is the appropriate response in approximately 75% of situations."

SIXTEEN

Hardy got a call and had to leave right after we finished with the pie booth. We gave each other a hug goodbye after he loaded my apples, and he promised to get in touch later.

Once I was on the road, my thoughts whirled over the events of the day.

I had missed Hardy. So much that seeing him made my heart hurt all over again.

It was time to stop living in denial. Hardy was worth all of my doubts about the future, about getting to know his daughter. This was my fear and no one else's, and if I wanted him in my life, it was worth seeing if my fear was unfounded or if I needed to walk away from him for good.

The decision lifted something heavy I'd carried for a while. For the first time in a long time, I felt lighter and much surer of the future.

Now that Alice was in town, it would be much easier to keep an eye on her. I still didn't think she was the culprit, but Daniel seemed to lean that way, so I'd keep her in the running.

The first thing I did when I got home was change into comfortable lounge clothes and wash off two pounds of apples for pie.

Once I had the music going, I tied my hair up, washed my hands, and started baking.

There was something cathartic about being in the kitchen on a fall day with the windows open and Amos Lee playing in the background. Notes of cinnamon and clove floated in the air, and I had hot cocoa simmering on the stove, and fresh whipped cream chilling in the fridge.

The only thing that would have made this better was someone to share it with. Maybe I'd bring Hardy a piece of pie tomorrow.

I smiled at the thought and peeked in the oven at the pie one more time. Noticing the crust was perfectly golden, and the filling bubbled over the top, I slid on some potholders and took it out of the oven to place on a trivet.

Ten minutes later, I was curled on the couch with a cup of hot chocolate topped with a mountain of whipped cream waiting for the pie to cool just enough for me to cut a slice.

A knock on the door ruined my silence. Sighing, I set my mug down and padded to the door.

To my surprise, Cole stood outside. He wore a cream-colored pullover and a pair of light-wash jeans with loafers and held a battered leather briefcase.

I held open the door. "Cole. Everything okay?"

He swept in, stopped, and inhaled. "Pie."

It was almost time to cut anyway. "Want a slice?"

He headed straight to the kitchen. "Yes, please."

I made him a cup of cocoa and dished up two slices of pie, topping them with whipped cream.

Cole cut into his the second I slid it over and groaned as he chewed.

"That bad?" I asked lightly.

"I received a tip this morning about Daniel Jensen."

My fork froze in mid-air.

"What kind of tip?"

"The kind you were hoping to avoid."

I closed my eyes and let out a deep exhale. "Anonymous?"

"Electronic voice."

"They must not know we're friends," I mused. If they had, they wouldn't have called Cole.

"Lucky break, I think."

"Did they give you a time limit?" So far, whoever this was seemed amateurish. They were sitting on a potential, if not false, goldmine, but they were more concerned about Daniel giving the money to them instead of anyone else. Maybe because they didn't want anyone else to know who they were?

"Forty-eight hours."

"Thank you for coming to me with this."

Cole snorted and ran a hand through his mussed blond hair. "This is what I get for having friends," he muttered.

"Breaking this story would catapult my career into the stratosphere."

I grinned, even though I felt a little bad for him. "Friends who make you pie. It will all even out eventually. But also, Daniel isn't guilty. Not of this one."

Cole took another bite of his pie, chewing thoughtfully. "What makes you so sure?"

"Instinct," I answered. "Daniel isn't quite what I thought he was, but his talent is real." If this turned out to be true, I think I'd hang my investigating hat up for good.

Cole frowned. "Oh? Trouble in paradise?"

"No paradise to begin with. We're still friends."

He held up his hands at my warning look. "Fine. I won't pry."

"Good. Then I won't tease you about Fletcher."

Cole coughed, choking on his pie. "Dirty move, Dakota."

I grinned at him, laughing when he glared. "What do you think I should do next?"

"Besides find out who this is and stop it before someone steals the scoop of my career?"

"Yes," I said dryly, sipping on my cocoa. I told him everything I'd found out so far. Cole listened intently, perking up when I mentioned Alice.

"She's in Silverwood?"

When I nodded, he made a hmm noise. "It's interesting she chose to come out here. I wonder if she's scared about being revealed."

"It seems more like she's obsessed with Daniel and can't get enough of him."

"If she's guilty, it's both, isn't it?"

Good point. "Could it be more than one person?"

"Always," Cole agreed. "You have someone who used to live around here and was involved with Daniel. There's the crazy fan lady..." He frowned.

"Jane," I supplied.

Cole snapped his fingers. "Yes. Jane. Then you have Alice sniffing around Daniel again. Could they all be working together?"

"I don't think Peter is involved. He had no idea what I was talking about when we talked."

"Maybe Jane and Alice?"

"How would I figure that out? I've never seen them together. Jane never mentioned anything about plagiarism. She came by wanting an early copy of his release and got angry when I wouldn't give her one, but she's never accused him of stealing anyone else's work."

"Do you think Jane is smart enough to put this all together?"

I set my fork down. "I don't know her well enough to decide. Every time I had to deal with her, she's been volatile and pushy. Intellect hasn't really been involved."

"What about Alice?" Cole scooped up the last bit of his pie.

"I don't know her either. She seems smitten with Daniel, but I haven't spent more than five minutes with her."

Cole nodded thoughtfully. "How much longer until you have your official license?"

"I'm expecting the email any day now."

"Good. How about an old-fashioned stakeout? It's been a while since I've done one, but I'm up for training a young'un."

"I'm as old as you are."

Cole gasped. "Old. How dare you?"

I thought about it. "You want to follow Jane?"

"Both. I'm not willing to give the scoop up, so it's in both of our best interests to solve this case. I'm willing to give your instincts the benefit of the doubt and believe Daniel isn't guilty, but I'll be darned if I let a tip like this slip through my fingers. So...bring snacks and pie, and make sure you pee before we go."

I blinked. "Tonight?"

Cole rose and took another swig of his cocoa. "Yup. Dress warm. We can't keep the vehicle running."

"You bringing the coffee if I bring the snacks?"

"One thermos. Coffee is a diuretic and makes you pee, so you better really want some java because you might be squatting toward the back of the car if you have to go during the stakeout."

"Cole!"

"Crime waits for no bladder," he said sagely. Cole winked, grabbed his briefcase, and sailed out the door. "I'll swing by and get you around seven. Thanks for the pie!" he called back.

Shaking my head, I locked the door after him.

A stakeout. Excitement uncurled in my belly. My very first one.

Cool.

I rushed to the bedroom to figure out something to wear.

SEVENTEEN

I shot off a quick text to Hardy letting him know I'd be with Cole and why.

He messaged me back almost immediately. *A stakeout? Who?*

I told him my suspicions.

Just be careful. I'm taking Izzy to the park a little later. Bundle up!

Let me know when you're back home safe.

My heart warmed. He didn't warn me away from doing it or try to force his opinion on me. All he said was to be careful and keep him posted.

I will.

My shoes sat right by the front door, along with my purse and a bag of snacks. I'd tucked my dark hair into a black beanie cap and removed all my jewelry. Wearing a black, long-sleeved shirt and a pair of black leggings, I looked like a cat burglar.

The knock came close to seven on the dot. I opened the door to see Cole wearing the exact same thing he'd worn earlier.

Taking one look at me, he burst out laughing. "Are we robbing someone tonight?" he said. "Or no. I got it. I'm lowering you down through the ceiling to steal the Declaration of Independence."

My jaw dropped. "Cole! Shouldn't we both be wearing dark clothes?" I poked him in the chest. "You're going to stick out like a sore thumb!"

"Relax, I have a dark jacket in the car. Besides, we don't want to look like we're spying. We want to look like we're hanging out and having a nice conversation." He rolled his eyes. "So go put on a normal shirt or something."

I stomped back to the bedroom and switched out my shirt for a green sweatshirt. The beanie came off next, and I tied my hair into a low ponytail.

"Better," he remarked when I came out of the room.

"I'm not sharing my snacks with you," I grumbled.

"How about with Fletcher?" he asked, his eyes twinkling.

"Fletcher?"

"She's in the car."

I made an oooooh noise. Cole waved an annoyed hand at me. "Stop. She's an adrenaline junkie and wanted to come. Don't read more into it than what it is." But I heard the hopeful note in his voice.

"I'm sure she wanted to come for more than one

reason," I said and backed away before Cole could punch my arm.

I laughed and waved my beanie at him. "I'm taking this just in case."

Cole bent down and grabbed the snacks. "Don't forget your grappling hook," he quipped as he stepped outside.

"Cole and Fletcher sitting in the tree," I sang quietly.

"*Dakota*," Cole hissed.

I cracked up laughing and followed him outside.

Fletcher and Cole made a good team, I decided. She refused to take the front seat, claiming she was a third wheel, and the real stakeout team was me and Cole. I sat in the front as Cole drove through town, stopping at a retro cafe with an outdoor sitting area.

"Her social media is public," Fletcher said, noticing my confused look. "She comes here once a week for trivia night."

"This town has trivia nights?" I loved trivia, but Daniel preferred chess, and Hardy never offered to play games unless I brought them out and strong-armed him.

"You need to get out more," Cole said.

"I'll get her there," Fletcher promised.

"Two martini limit," I muttered.

Fletcher's laugh was merry.

"Are you sure she's here?" I asked.

"She confirmed earlier." Cole glanced at me. "Do you know what she drives?"

I chewed on my lip. "Small car. I can't remember what kind. I think it's blue?"

Cole and Fletcher scanned the parking lot. "That one?" he asked, pointing to a row of cars. A small dark-blue, four-door sedan was parked between a small SUV and a pickup truck. I squinted. "I think so. Can you see any stickers?"

Fletcher craned her neck around. "Maybe? It's too dark to tell."

"I'll check the restaurant's account again." Cole pulled his cell out, the artificial glow turning his face a sickly blue. He scrolled for a moment, tapping something before exclaiming, "Yup. She's here. And way too excited about wizard school trivia."

Fletcher huffed. "Bet I could crush her. We had the best trivia back home. I came in the top three every time I went."

"I'm not too shabby at trivia. Maybe we can go sometime."

"There you go, Dakota. Way to make friends."

Fletcher reached over the seat and shoved Cole in the shoulder. "Don't be mean to my new BFF." She winked at me. "I'll call you about trivia. I think this place has themed nights, so let's make sure we pick one we're both good at."

"Deal," I said. "How long until it's over?"

Cole checked his cell. "About twenty minutes. Even if she doesn't leave right away, the restaurant closes half an hour after trivia ends, so she won't be too long."

"In twenty minutes, I want you to fork over the coffee."

Fletcher leaned over the seat. "You brought coffee?"

"I insisted. And I have snacks." I picked the canvas bag up and handed it to her.

She grabbed it and pawed through it like a hungry raccoon, crowing when she pulled out a Snickers bar. "Haaaaa!" Fletcher waved it around like a trophy.

Cole eyed her in the mirror, a soft smile playing over his lips.

Ooooh. He had it bad for her. "Did you bring more than one?" he asked.

I shook my head.

Fletcher tore open the wrapper with her teeth and took a massive bite.

"Haha," she said through a mouthful of nuts and chocolate.

Cole rolled his eyes, but I could tell he wasn't annoyed. He was enamored.

Tamping my smile down, I took the bag back from her, rummaged through it, and pulled out an Almond Joy.

"Want this?"

Cole snatched it out of my hand. "You bring good snacks."

"Put that on my tombstone," I said.

Fletcher chuckled. "Snickers on a stakeout. Last time I went on one, my partner brought stale cheese crackers."

I grimaced. "Gross."

"Exactly. When I tried to tell him he needed to up his snack game, he got offended."

"That's why I put Dakota in charge of snacks," Cole

said. "I knew she'd spring for the good stuff. Though I don't smell pie."

"Pie doesn't travel well. I'll have more if you want to pop by in a few days. The market guy had a great selection of apples, so I bought twenty pounds."

Fletcher choked on her candy bar. "Pounds?" she wheezed.

"I really love apple pie."

Cole laughed. The conversation ebbed and flowed until we fell into a companionable silence. When twenty minutes had passed, Cole poured me a steaming cup of coffee already fixed with cream and sugar.

"Me, too," Fletcher said, waving a small Yeti cup at him.

Cole obliged her and poured himself one as well.

A few minutes later, people began to pour out of the restaurant. Cole sat up straighter. I leaned forward, keeping my eyes peeled for Jane.

"Do you see her?" Fletcher murmured.

"Not yet."

Cole handed Fletcher his phone. "Here. Forgot to show you a picture."

Fletcher scanned it and handed it back. "She's young. You think she's the one?" She let out a sigh. "I don't see it."

"Just from a picture?" Cole asked.

"She doesn't have those crazy eyes," Fletcher remarked.

I craned my head to stare at her. "What does that mean?"

"You know. Crazy eyes. You can look at some people and see the crazy shining in their eyes, and you know you aren't dealing with someone who has all their marbles. She doesn't have that."

"She acts pretty crazy when she comes in," I said.

"Is she an author or a fan?" Fletcher asked.

"Both from what I can tell. She's mentioned working on a book, but she's a big reader, and always purchases Daniel's books on the day of the release. Since I announced the signing, she's been more...annoying than usual."

"Has she ever said why she's so obsessed with him?"

I shook my head. "No. She's never been aggressive until a few days ago. When I wouldn't hand those books over, I thought I might have to kick her out of the store over the way she reacted."

"There," Cole said, his voice low and urgent. "She shouldn't look this way since her car is away from us but try not to make any sudden movements."

"Like jumping jacks?" Fletcher asked dryly.

"Hilarious," Cole said. "Just stay still. Next time I'm doing a stakeout on my own."

"Then you won't get Dakota's candy bars," Fletcher remarked. "I'll have them all to myself."

"Shhh," Cole hissed.

Jane didn't do anything suspicious or abnormal. She carried a canvas bag with her, something that looked like a large notebook sticking out of the top. No one walked with her or even spoke to her, so if she was with a team, they either hadn't left yet or walked out without her.

I felt a little sad for her.

"Are we going to follow?" I asked Cole.

He nodded. "We'll wait for a couple of cars to get ahead of us before we pull out, so she won't expect anything."

"Very clandestine," Fletcher said from the back.

Jane got in her car and started it up. Several cars pulled out, and she followed behind.

Cole pulled out behind a small pickup truck, keeping Jane in his sight, but staying well away from her vehicle. We drove in silence for the next fifteen minutes or so until Jane pulled onto a side road. Cole drove straight past it.

"That road is a straight shot for a while. I'll turn around and follow her in a minute."

I nodded, my heart beating like a drum.

"Do you know where Alice is staying?" Cole asked.

"No, though I assume with Daniel. His house is massive." The thought didn't bother me like I thought it might.

"That guy is very bad at keeping an ex-girlfriend." Cole shook his head. "This is going to blow up in his face."

Fletcher patted Cole on the shoulder. "You should know, buddy."

Even in the dark, I could see Cole's cheeks go red.

I burst out laughing. "What did you do?"

"This is not the time for this," he growled.

"We're all stuck in a small space together. I can't think of a better time," I said sweetly.

Fletcher snorted.

"Dakota. Please." There was a strangled note of desperation in his voice that made me feel bad for him.

I huffed. "Fine. Keep your secrets." I glanced at Fletcher, who mouthed, *I'll tell you later.*

Apparently, we'd moved from acquaintances to friends. I gave her a thumbs up, ignoring Cole's dark look.

He turned onto the road Jane went down. Her taillights reflected in the distance. "There aren't many houses on this road. No business either."

"Hmm. Will it be suspicious with us behind her?" I asked.

"Not if we stay far enough behind and don't draw attention to ourselves," Cole said.

"We can always pretend we're lost if something happens," Fletcher added.

"She'll recognize me." Jane was in the bookstore often enough that she would peg me in an instant. "Just be careful."

The taillights disappeared.

Cole let out a muffled curse.

"Did she turn?" Fletcher asked.

"If she didn't, she's onto us," Cole murmured.

Fletcher put a hand on his shoulder. "Don't slow down. Maintain speed. If something happens, you know how to get out of it."

I gave her a considering look. "Have you two gotten out of things like this before?"

Fletcher shrugged. "Most of our stories don't involve any danger. They're downright boring. But every once in a while, we find ourselves in a real pickle. Both of us know how to drive a vehicle well."

"Well?" I laughed.

"If Jane is stopped in the middle of the road with an unwelcome surprise, Cole will get us out of it," was all she said.

I sat back in my seat, my heart wildly beating. "Surely not Jane," I said faintly.

"I never underestimate anyone," Fletcher said. "It's probably nothing."

"Famous last words," Cole said ominously.

He maintained his speed but turned on his brights. We drove for the next minute until Cole let out a relieved breath. "She turned," he said. "Her car is in the driveway of the house to the left."

Cole kept driving, but I craned my neck to view the place. Nothing looked odd or strange. It was just a simple country house with the porch light left on.

"I'll drive for a couple more minutes, then turn around. I think this is her residence."

"You should be able to find the address if you pull up Google Earth," Fletcher said.

"Did we waste our time tonight?" I wondered aloud.

Headlights popped up behind us. Cole stiffened in his seat.

"Maybe not," Fletcher said, turning to look behind us. "It's too dark to see anything. I think you should find a place to turn into and turn off your lights."

"I'm not turning into a random driveway and sitting there with the lights off like I'm about to rob the place," Cole said.

"Not a driveway. A wooded area. There should be a few places to turn off."

"There's a crossroad a mile or so ahead. I'll turn down that road and see what happens."

We drove in tense silence for a while. When the headlights disappeared, Fletcher snapped her fingers. "What are the odds they turned into Jane's driveway?"

"High," I said thoughtfully. "How soon can we turn around?"

"We should give it at least five minutes," Cole said. The road came up, and we turned, but Cole didn't keep going. He pulled off to the shoulder, put the vehicle in park, and turned the lights off. "There are no houses out this way, so we should be fine to sit here for a little while."

Once we were back on the road, Cole reduced his speed a little. As we drove past Jane's house, we spotted a little red Mustang sitting in the driveway.

"Perfect car for a socialite, isn't it?" Cole mused.

I groaned.

"Guess this wasn't a waste after all, was it?" I said.

"Before we jump to conclusions, we need to ensure this is actually Alice's car," Fletcher added.

I sighed and reached for the thermos. "Anyone want a top up?"

Two cups were shoved at me almost instantaneously.

EIGHTEEN

Cole and Fletcher dropped me off, waving once I stepped through my doorway. She'd stolen most of my snacks, so the canvas bag I brought was almost empty when I brought it in.

I stretched and groaned at the pop in my back, relieved to be home. Before I did anything else, I headed straight to the kitchen and cut myself another sliver of pie.

Pie was always good for thinking, and I had a lot of thinking to do.

Alerting Daniel might put him in danger if Alice was staying with him. If I asked him what kind of car she drove, he'd want to know why and would pry until I gave up the information.

I texted him. *Mind if I stop by tomorrow to give you an update?*

It was the best way to figure out what she drove without alerting him. I didn't think she was harmful in a violent way. Definitely harmful to his career, but if I were careful, he wouldn't have to worry about anything because I planned to nail both of them very soon.

The moment I figured out how they were working together.

Sure. Mind picking up some lunch?

We made a plan to meet around one.

Will Alice be there?

His response took longer to come this time.

Yes. Is that an issue?

Nope! Just wanted to ask if she wanted anything for lunch.

She doesn't eat on a normal schedule. Intermittent fasting or something. Whatever her diet of the month is.

I didn't touch that one with a ten-foot pole.

See you tomorrow!

Night, Dakota.

I put my phone down and pulled my notebook out, jotting down everything I'd learned so far.

All in all, today was productive. I wish I'd had the entire day off without working on any cases, but I wouldn't have discovered the Alice/Jane connection if I had.

Poppy came up and rubbed between my ankles. I reached down and picked her up.

"Hey, you. You've been hiding a lot lately. Everything okay?"

She meowed and headbutted me. I rose, taking her with me, and checked her food and watering machine. She'd eaten tonight, which was good, so there was no issue with her appetite. Maybe she just didn't want to spend time with anyone for a little bit. It wasn't unusual for her. I carried her back over to my notebook and tapped it with my index finger.

"Want to figure this out for me?"

Poppy stared at it, then looked up at me and meowed again.

"Exactly," I said and sighed. "It's a real mess." I stared at my notes for another ten minutes or so, snuggling with Poppy, until my eyes started to blur.

I double checked the locks, shut the lights off and took her into the bedroom. She had a bed here and in the living room.

"Ready for bed?" I put her in her bed and pulled her little pumpkin blanket over her. She promptly rolled onto her back and blinked at me with her strange chartreuse eyes.

"I'm wiped. Want to come with me to Daniel's tomorrow?"

She meowed again.

"It's settled then. But you have to be nice at his house, okay?"

Poppy blinked at me. She never promised to be nice.

That was far beyond my little kitty.

THE NEXT MORNING, we were on the road by eleven. Poppy curled in her hammock and watched the scenery stream by. Food steamed in the passenger seat, making my mouth water. We'd chosen a local Japanese restaurant we hadn't tried yet but had good reviews.

Daniel's house came into view just as we crested the hill, an imposing modern mansion that took my breath away.

The gates opened as I pulled up, courtesy of a small sticker Daniel had given me after we'd met for chess several times. I pulled into the driveway and parked.

Right next to a small red Mustang.

Daniel met me at the front door with Alice plastered to his side. He gave me a pained smile and held the door open.

Alice wore a bright smile and an even brighter hot pink top with a pair of cream-colored cords and matching flats. Her hair was perfectly done in a neat chignon and her makeup looked flawless.

"Hello," I greeted and breezed past them both, heading straight to the kitchen to put the food down. Poppy leapt out of my arms and headed to the living room, where she sat on her haunches and stared at all of us.

Alice gave her a weird look but shook her head and followed behind. "Do you always bring your cat with you?"

"When she wants to come." Poppy meowed in agreement.

Alice didn't say anything, but I could tell she wasn't comfortable with her presence.

But Daniel liked Poppy, and that was all that mattered.

Ignoring both of them, I took all the food out of the bags and put Daniel's order into a neat pile. "Alice, I'm happy to share what I brought if you're hungry. Daniel mentioned you fasted?"

She nodded and patted her slim stomach. "Yes. Thanks for the offer, but I don't eat before two."

If I didn't eat by nine, I turned into a raging bear. "I can set some aside for you if you'd like it for later."

"No, thank you. Too much salt and fat for me." Her smile sharpened.

"Alice," Daniel said quietly.

To my great delight, Poppy hissed from the living room.

I bit down my smile and opened my silverware packet. "More for me, then."

Daniel gave me an apologetic glance as he picked up his food. "Want to eat in the library?"

Alice sucked in a gasp. "In the library?" She shook her head. "No. Eat in the kitchen."

Daniel's eyes flashed with anger. "Dakota and I always eat in the library when she's here."

Her voice turned plaintive. "But Daniel, it's such a nice area." She trailed her fingers up his arm. "It'd be a shame to spoil it with fast food containers, wouldn't it?"

I tried really hard to be the kind of person who didn't judge others. Being human made it impossible to prevent being judgmental completely, though. While I didn't say a word because this situation wasn't my business, I turned away and got myself a glass of water, keeping the faucet on a little longer than necessary while they spoke in hushed whispers.

When I turned back around, color had bloomed high on Alice's cheeks. Her lips were pinched in fury, and she turned away in a huff, stomping through the house until she disappeared.

I winced. "Daniel, I—"

He waved my words away. "No. Sometimes, I have trouble with boundaries. Alice is a good example." His smile didn't reach his eyes. "She's packing up and should be gone before you leave today."

"Are you sure? I can go."

"No." He picked up his food. "Come on. Let's go to the library."

After Poppy followed us in, Daniel shut the door behind us and sank into his seat once he set his food down. A long, aggrieved sigh escaped him.

I covered my mouth with my hand to hide a smile.

"She's the worst," he whispered. "I wonder if this is how women feel after they have a baby."

I laughed. "You mean the phenomena where they forget all about the reflux, hemorrhoids, childbirth pain, and eighteen years of financial responsibility and have another one to restart the cycle?"

Daniel snorted. "Yes. Exactly. I'd forgotten the pain of having Alice in my life until she came back."

"The difference is kids love you unconditionally."

"Alice is very much conditional," he said dryly.

I glanced at the door. "Can she hear us?"

He shook his head. "No. Soundproofed." A faint smile crossed his lips. "The recent events have made me even more paranoid than usual. I've upgraded some things in the house."

I opened the container and speared a piece of chicken with my fork. "Alice is working with someone on my suspect list. I don't know how it all fits together yet, but she's involved."

He sat back in his chair and studied me. "I guess it's a good thing she's leaving then," he said lightly. "How did you figure it out?"

"Stakeout last night. We followed Jane home and spotted Alice's vehicle following her."

"You didn't come here to brief me, did you? You came to check out Alice."

I smiled in response.

"I suppose it's hard to miss a red Mustang, isn't it?" Daniel chuckled. "What are the next steps?"

"All I have to figure out is how they're working together."

"I'd like to know why," Daniel said.

I clicked my tongue. "That's not part of the deal, Mr. Jensen."

He laughed. "Fair enough." Daniel picked up his fork and dug in. "Let's table this for a while. I'm starving."

"Good with me," I said. "There's not much else left to say anyway."

NINETEEN

Apprehension filled me when it came time to leave the library. Daniel chuckled when I started tiptoeing to the door.

"She's gone," he said from the hallway.

I let out a relieved breath as I scooped up Poppy. "Expect this to get much worse before it gets better."

"I'll call my agent as soon as I walk you out."

Daniel walked me to my car and pulled the door open for me. His bark of alarm made me take an involuntary step back.

"Daniel?"

His muttered curse took me by surprise. "You can take one of my cars while I have yours cleaned and repaired."

He stepped in front of me to block my view, but I pushed him out of the way. To my dismay, a white liquid pooled in my seats, on the floor, and dripped from the air conditioning vents.

A choked gasp escaped me. "Harmless?" I croaked.

Daniel laid a hand on my shoulder. "I'm so sorry. I never expected she would do something like this." He led me back inside and sat me in a comfortable chair in the living room. "Is there anyone you want me to call? I can get you a vehicle if you want."

"Hardy. Please." I cleared my throat and looked away. He was always the first one I thought of.

He stared at me for a long moment, eyes glimmering with emotion, before nodding once. "I see." Daniel turned and pulled his cell phone from his pocket.

I tuned out his murmured words and looked out the window at the lovely scene before me. Daniel's mansion was picturesque, every window set at a point outside with a lovely view.

I rose and let myself outside, tugging my sweater closer as I wandered into the middle of his garden. Poppy followed close behind.

A warm hand on my shoulder sometime later jerked me out of my reverie.

"Dakota."

I tilted my face up to see Hardy's concerned expression. He crouched down beside me. "Are you okay?"

"I'm going to need a new car," I said faintly.

His jaw tightened. "No. Mr. Jensen has assured me he will see your car restored to perfect condition."

My sigh sounded heavy. "I've needed one for a while. I almost wish I had never received that money. Having it cripples me."

Hardy sat beside me in the cold grass, tucking me under his arm. "It's mental. Money is freeing. Have you spoken to an advisor or anything yet?"

"I'm afraid to. It's sitting there taunting me."

Hardy chuckled. "You'll figure it out. I'll help you if you want."

A tear slipped down my face. "Hardy?"

"Hmm?"

"I love you." He was always there for me, no matter what happened between us. Hardy was the one solid thing I had in my life that had never once let me down.

He stilled. Silence stretched between us before he let out a slow breath. "Well, that's good, because I never stopped loving you." Hardy pressed a kiss to my temple. "Ready to go?"

I nodded and let him help me up. Poppy twined between his ankles, and he bent to scoop her up. My cat nuzzled her face against his chest as he navigated us outside.

Daniel leaned against my vehicle. When he spotted us, he straightened. "I'm having it towed to the shop in the next few minutes."

I nodded.

"Should we file a police report?" he asked.

Hardy said nothing, leaving the decision up to me. "Not right now. I want her to think she's getting away with it for now."

Daniel rubbed his eyes. "I can't begin to apologize to you for this—"

"Don't worry about it," I said wearily. "I'll put it on my bill."

He snorted. "You won't have to. I'll settle it way before then." His eyes met Hardy's, and a silent conversation passed between them. "I'll leave you to it then." Daniel shoved his hands in his pockets and turned to walk into the house.

Hardy settled me into his vehicle. Moments later, we were on the way back to Silverwood Hollow.

He walked me to the door, holding the screen open while I fidgeted with the lock. When I finally got it open and lowered Poppy to the ground, who shot inside like a rocket, he took a step back.

I yanked him inside by the tie, making him belly laugh.

"Pie?" I asked.

"You know the answer to that," he said in a low, gruff voice.

Smiling to myself, I led him to a stool, sat him down, and dished him up a piece. Then I put on a fresh pot of coffee and marveled at the fact that I had Hardy sitting in my kitchen again.

"I missed you," I admitted.

"I'm worried about how we are going to handle Izzy with this. How *you* will," he admitted.

"Me too," I said. "When it all happened, I was stunned. I didn't know how to deal with it. But living without you has been awful and confusing and heartbreaking." I looked away. "And I don't want to do it anymore."

His fork clattered to his plate. Hardy rose to his feet, swept me in his arms, and pressed his lips against mine.

I melted into his embrace, running my fingers through his dark, silky hair.

And when he kicked open the door to my bedroom, I didn't protest.

"TELL ME EVERYTHING." Hardy sat on my reading chair, balancing a plate of Marsala cream pasta and broccoli.

"Everything?" I frowned at him. "There's a lot to go through."

He shifted, setting his plate down and picking up his glass of wine. "I've been thinking about things lately," he admitted. "Life is about people. Family, friends, others you love." He sighed and studied the ruby colored Pinot Noir in his glass. "The last thing I want to do is live a life of regret. Izzy changed everything for me. Losing you did, too. I want to do something that matters."

My mouth fell open. "Hardy," I said after a moment. "You do. You're important to this town."

"Yes, but I want to be home for my daughter at a reasonable hour. I want to know I did the best I could for someone without getting caught up in red tape."

I huffed a laugh. "Sounds like you want to be a private investigator."

His eyes met mine.

I blinked, the possibilities unfurling in front of me like the petals of a rose.

"Oh," I breathed.

Hardy shook his head. "I've been thinking about it for a while, hoping we would one day get back together. But this is a lot, and it's all at once, and we have no idea how you and Izzy will get along." His voice shook with emotion.

I went over to him, took his plate away, and slid into his lap. "Yes," was all I said.

His arms tightened around my waist. "Yes?"

"Of course," I breathed.

"We should take it one day at a time. And nothing official until things...move. Substantially."

"Whatever you say, Detective Cavanaugh."

His laugh vibrated my collarbone.

"Now. Tell me everything about this case."

I laughed and tightened my arms around his neck. "As you wish."

We talked long into the night. By the time dawn stretched its fingers over the town, Hardy and I had a solid plan.

And an ice cream date with him and his little girl.

I shoved a mug of coffee at him with a grunt. Hardy snorted and caught my fingers. "I forgot how cranky you are when you're short on sleep."

"Mmmmf," I said in response.

He laughed and caught me by the hips, pulling him into the open space between his knees. "I have to go get Izzy from my sister's house. She loves a sleepover, but I don't like disrupting her routine too often. See you tonight?"

I nodded. "I'll meet you there." A knot of nerves had bundled in my stomach over the prospect of officially meeting his daughter. I'd seen her once before I walked out on him, but I'd never had a single conversation with her.

I loved her dad so much that I was willing to do whatever it took to make it work.

Whatever happened, I finally knew Hardy and I would do our best to make it work.

TWENTY

Alice made herself scarce. Her family name gave her a lot of power in many places, but this wasn't a major city. It was a small town with a detective who didn't take kindly to behavior like hers.

Although he wasn't officially an employee or contractor with my P.I. business yet, Hardy offered to let me know if he spotted Alice or Jane—an offer I took him up on.

When I stepped outside with my coffee, I saw a car sitting in my driveway with the keys in the ignition, and a note on the steering wheel.

Your car should be ready in about a week. Take this one while you wait. My deepest apologies.

Shaking my head, I went back in to get ready for the day.

I ran by the bookstore once I had enough coffee to fuel

an RV in me and greeted Harper as she rang up a customer.

She smiled happily and waved when she spotted me. I handed her a latte I'd stopped and bought for her.

"The boss brings gifts!" she said with a laugh.

"How's it going? Anything you need my help with?"

She reached under the desk and pulled up a manila folder. "Resumes for the assistant positions. I separated them by immediate yes for interviews, maybes, and absolutely not."

I blinked. "Who were the absolutely nots?"

She snorted. "You'll see."

I opened the file and flipped right to the reject pile. She had everything clipped with color-appropriate paperclips, which made me chuckle: green for the yes pile, yellow for the maybe pile, and red for the no. "Have you called anyone for interviews?"

"Not yet. I wanted you to review the resumes before I made any calls."

"I'll look at them and give you my thoughts, but I trust you. If we ever have to hire anyone again, I trust you to make the decision."

Her expression brightened. "Thank you!"

I pulled up a chair and started flipping through the piles. Harper straightened up as I worked. "Has Jane come back in?"

Harper shook her head. "I haven't seen her since the last time."

"And no weird phone calls?"

"No weirder than usual," she said with a chuckle.

"Good."

The bell jingled announcing a new presence. Harper's eyebrows lifted. "For you, I think," she murmured.

I turned my head to see Hardy in the doorway. At my expression, Harper sucked in a breath. "Oh thank goodness," she quietly breathed.

I laughed.

She leaned forward. "I like Daniel, but Hardy looks at you like you're the sun."

Harper reached over and squeezed my hand before she waved at Hardy and slipped off to the back.

He filled the space with his presence. Bright blue eyes found mine. "Are we alone?" he growled.

I nodded.

Hardy took a few steps over, put his arm around me, and planted a steaming kiss on my lips.

When he pulled away, I swayed. "Well," I breathed. "What was that for?"

He grinned, the sight of it tugging at my heart. "Just because."

I cleared my throat. "I hope *just because* happens a lot more than occasionally."

He chuckled and pulled up a stool to sit beside me. "I can't stay long." Hardy pushed a folder he carried over to me. "This is all I could pull up without getting myself into trouble."

I blinked. "About Alice?"

"Jane. Alice is a landmine. She's a socialite with a massive social media presence and parents with a ton of money. I know better than to look into her without probable cause."

"She puts everything on social media anyway," I said dryly. "I could probably trace her for the last five years if I concentrated on her Instagram account long enough."

Hardy laughed and rose from his seat. "You ready for tonight?"

I nodded, tears filling my eyes. "I hope she likes me."

He brushed a curl away from my face. "She's going to love you."

Hardy smiled and left, the jingling bell announcing his absence.

Ice cream. It was only ice cream. I could do this.

Harper came out a few minutes later beaming. "You're back together?"

At my nod, she clapped her hands together. "I'm so happy!"

"I'm meeting his daughter tonight."

Her expression sobered. "Oh. Wow. Goodness. Big step. Are you ready?"

I inhaled and closed my eyes. "I think so. How can a kid be this intimidating?"

Harper laughed. "No matter what age they are, it's always difficult meeting someone else's child. You love him, don't you?"

I nodded.

"Then there's even more pressure." She shook her head and slung an arm around me. "But you're amazing. How could anyone not love you?"

I laughed. "Let's hope. We're going for ice cream."

Harper nodded. "Good. It's simple and quick. You can get the lay of the land, and she doesn't feel pressure to spend too much time with you. Plus, there's rocky road involved. There can be no mutual dislike when chocolate ice cream and marshmallows are involved."

"I like your logic."

Harper waved her hand like it was a magic wand. "Kids are complicated but simple." Her face softened. "Just be you, Dakota. That's all you can do."

We smiled at each other. I pushed the folder back over. "Whoever you want to hire, I approve. Put them on a 90-day probationary period and, depending on their experience, sixteen to eighteen bucks an hour. Sounds good?"

Her eyes widened. "That much?"

I shrugged. "I assume you're going to work them a lot?"

Harper laughed. "During training, yes. I'm not sure after that."

"Parttime. I'd say no more than 20 hours per week. You want to hire two?"

Harper nodded. "Perfect," I said. "You can split them however you want, though I'd say equal for now. If one doesn't work out, we can talk about it later." I tapped the folder. "I trust your judgment. Just don't hire Jane."

"No kidding," Harper said with a laugh. She tucked

the folder under her arm. "Interviews the day after tomorrow?"

"Sounds good to me." I rose and reached out to give her a hug. "Thanks, Harper. I'm glad we met."

She hugged me and patted me on the back. "Me too. Now go catch a criminal."

"Two," I said ominously. "I think."

"Oooh," Harper said. "You're a regular caped crusader."

"That's me," I said lightly. "Sans cape."

"However you do it, it's working."

I waved goodbye and sailed out the door, the folder Hardy gave me tucked safely into my bag.

Before I did anything else, I swung by the house and grabbed Poppy.

She didn't protest, instead curling up in her hammock when I took her to the car and eyeing me with bright eyes. "Ready for a stakeout?"

She didn't respond, but her posture was alert and ready.

We drove past Jane's house first, but her car wasn't there. Disappointed but not surprised, Poppy and I drove through town to see if we could spot her vehicle. When nothing jumped out at us, I grabbed a coffee and sat in the parking lot with the engine running while I perused the file Hardy had given me.

"Huh." Her name really was Jane. Jane Mariah Coleman, to be exact. Not White like she told me before. There wasn't a lot of info on the printout Hardy had given me.

Her full name, age, address, and last three workplaces. I already knew her address. She was twenty-four and worked at a place called Repairs4U. It was impossible to tell what kind of business that was, though I assumed it was something with electronics. She didn't look much like a mechanic.

I pulled up the address on my phone and drove across town until I spotted it. The shop was located in a small, nondescript shopping center, sandwiched between a nail place and a dry cleaner. A blue four-door sedan sat parked in the front. I recognized it from our stakeout the other night. Parking might reveal me, so I slowly drove past it, straining to see inside the shop to no avail.

An elementary school loomed across the street, close to a small cafe and another shopping mall. I rarely came to this side of town because I had no reason to, but I always liked trying new places. The cafe was a convenient place to grab a bite and keep an eye on Jane's whereabouts.

I called in an order once I found a good parking spot that allowed me to keep an eye on Jane's parking lot. In less than ten minutes, a message dinged notifying me my food was ready for pickup. I dashed inside and paid, and when I got back to the car, the food smelled so good, even Poppy was curious about it. I took my time savoring the chef's special Benedict and hash browns, occasionally offering Poppy a small bite of the crispy potatoes.

When the door to the repair shop opened, revealing Jane, dressed in skinny jeans and an oversized black hoodie, I packed up my food, much to Poppy's distress. Jane went straight to her vehicle and headed out.

Fortunately, Silverwood Hollow wasn't exactly bustling around this area, so I was able to keep her in sight as I started my car and turned onto the highway a few cars after her.

To my surprise and frustration, Jane headed straight for Tattered Pages. I pulled in right after her, and waited a few minutes, giving her time to get inside the store and browse a little. Leaving Harper to deal with Jane felt cruel, but I wanted to see Jane and try to get her to crack, so I grabbed my purse and followed a few minutes later, gently setting Poppy on the ground when I walked in.

Harper and Jane stood at opposite sides of the register glaring at each other. I bit down my smile and walked up to them.

"Dakota!" Harper said cheerily, but I could hear the forced note in her voice.

"Hi, Harper." I stepped up beside Jane and nodded to her.

Jane frowned when she saw me. Harper was wonderful, but she had a softer heart than I did. "Can I help you with something?"

"I'm picking up an order." She flicked a hand at Harper. "But she said the register wasn't working and she won't let me look at it."

I gave her an odd look. "Why would she let you look at it?"

Jane threw her hands up. "Because that's what I do for a living!"

Color rose on Harper's cheeks at Jane's outburst. "It's the computer system. It won't process payments."

I reached over the counter and turned the monitor toward me. Sure enough it was frozen. Curious, I passed the keyboard over to Jane. "Can you do something about this?"

She rolled her eyes and took the keyboard. "Of course I can. Give me a second."

Pieces of the puzzle started locking together inside my brain. I watched Jane typing and clicking furiously. "Where's your router?"

I walked her to the back and watched her like a hawk while she messed with the device. Some things were beyond me. Mechanical, electrical, and anything to do with the Wi-Fi or internet. I knew books. I hired people like Jane to fix the other things for me because I was hopeless.

Jane rose and went back to the keyboard. She tapped away for a bit, and just like she promised, after a little while, the system was fixed, and Harper was able to ring her purchase up.

"Huh," Harper said when Jane was gone without an ounce of fanfare.

"Yeah," I agreed, watching as the woman tossed her bag inside the car and drove away. "Curious, isn't it?"

"What are you thinking?" Harper asked.

Jane reminded me of tangled Christmas lights.

Confusing and sometimes exasperating until you set them to rights. "I'm not sure yet, but that feels important, doesn't it?"

Harper's eyes narrowed. "Did you know she could do that?"

"I don't know much about Jane at all," I admitted.

But ever so slowly, an emerging picture was beginning to form in my mind.

TWENTY-ONE

Alice continued to make herself scarce. A check of her social media revealed her still pretending to have a great time in Silverwood Hollow. She posted a video of a barely tolerant Daniel and her inside of his kitchen while she cooked a barely recognizable dish she claimed was pasta.

Socialites. Rolling my eyes, I shut down the app and tried to figure out how I could find her.

When nothing came to me, I decided to ask my younger, cooler helper. "Harper?"

She looked up from her magazine. "Hmm?"

"If you were trying to find someone and only had their social media to track them, what would you do?"

Harper chewed on her lip for a moment. "It depends on how savvy they are. The vast majority of people don't realize how much info you can get on someone with a simple post. If the person I'm looking for is better about online safety, I look at their friend's social media. Try to find a pattern in her comments. Is there someone who comments on all or most of her posts? Figure out if it's a friend or a fan. If it's a friend, look at their social media. See if they've tagged the person and see if they've listed where they are."

I stared at Harper for a long moment. "That's genius. And frightening."

She lifted a shoulder. "It's one of the reasons I don't use social media much," she admitted.

I brought my phone over to her and pulled up Alice's profile. "I'm looking for her."

Harper peered at the profile. "Alice Merritt? Should be easy. She's constantly posting her whereabouts. This is a girl who loves to be seen."

"You know her?"

"No. She's somewhat of a local celebrity, though."

"Huh."

Harper laughed. "For people who follow pop culture, at least." She grinned up at me. "Here. Let's look at her most recent post."

When she saw the one with Daniel, her eyes widened a hair. "Interesting," she murmured. Harper clicked on the comments section and skimmed. "Her." She pointed to a username, *socialitekitty*. "I've seen her in photos with Alice before. Here, and in the newspaper."

"You follow her?"

Harper shrugged. "I do, but it's been a while since I've logged on." She clicked on the other profile. "You're in luck. This one is from today, though it's been about an hour. She's having lunch just down the road with Alice."

"What in the world?" I murmured to myself. "I'm getting rid of all my social media."

She laughed. "Yeah, it's both the greatest and the worst thing to ever happen to society."

I grabbed my purse and slung it over my shoulder. "I'm going to run over there and see if I can spot her."

"Did she do something?"

"Not sure yet. I want to know where she's staying so I can keep an eye on her."

Harper waved my phone. "She isn't staying with Daniel?"

"Not anymore."

"Oooh. Ominous." Harper wiggled her fingers.

"She vandalized my car and left before Hardy could get there."

Harper choked on her drink. "What?"

"Long story." I waved at her as I hurried to the door.

"You better have time soon!" Harper called as I stepped out.

Let's hope. Time was quickly running out for Daniel if it hadn't already.

Alice's little red Mustang sat in the parking lot of the cafe. Breathing a sigh of relief, I pulled in at the opposite end of the lot and parked my car facing her vehicle, turning my vehicle off to wait. She shouldn't be too much longer if they'd already been there for over an hour.

I hoped.

A podcast on my phone kept me from going stir-crazy while I waited. About half an hour later, Alice walked out with another dark-haired girl. Both held their cell phones up to their faces.

I snorted and wondered what in the world Daniel had seen in her, then promptly shoved that thought away. It was none of my business.

The two girls tossed their hair and fake laughed, eventually parting ways and heading to separate vehicles. I waited for Alice to pull out and followed her until she pulled into the driveway of a cute, Craftsman-style house right on the edge of town.

I knew for a fact this place was an Airbnb because it had thrown the entire town up in arms. Our town thrived on tourism, but no one wanted the family homes snatched up and turned into rentals for many reasons, the two most significant being the welfare of our townspeople and the potential collapse of the bed-and-breakfast and hotel industry we already had.

This single place had almost halted our real estate market because no one wanted their homes bought by investors. Even if they planned to move, Silverwood Hollow residents still loved the town and wanted the best for it.

I drove past without slowing down and pulled into a shopping strip parking lot about a quarter of a mile away.

Daniel's vehicle was a four-door sedan, nothing too flashy, but it was a Beemer, and we didn't have too many of those around here. I had to be careful for her not to notice me. She'd recognize me right away if I got too close.

Her vehicle was like a beacon, so I'd notice her if she was around town. My phone rang, the screen flashing Fletcher's name.

"Hey," I greeted.

"Dakota." Fletcher's voice was hushed.

I straightened. "What's wrong?"

"Where are you?"

"In a parking lot. I'm tailing Alice."

"Can you meet me?"

I already knew where Alice was staying, so leaving her wouldn't be an issue. "Where?"

Fletcher rattled off a fast-food restaurant near where I was. "Fifteen minutes?" she asked.

"You can't tell me over the phone?"

"No. I'll see you soon." She disconnected before I could say anything else.

Frowning, I put my cell back into the holder and pulled up the Airbnb website, doing a search around this area. The house Alice was staying in popped up, so I tried to book three days, starting tomorrow. It came back as already booked, so that gave me a good feeling Alice planned to stay put for a while. As far as everyone knew, the owner was losing money on this place with all the other establishments offering better deals and free meals to book with them.

Alice could afford to blow the money, and this place wasn't in the thick of downtown.

Satisfied I could find Alice again, I pulled out of the parking lot and headed to meet Fletcher.

TWENTY-TWO

Fletcher wore athletic attire and tied her flaming hair in a sloppy bun on top of her head. She wore no makeup and still attracted admiring glances even while slumped at her table.

Her expression brightened when she spotted me.

I sat across from her. "Everything okay?"

Fletcher looked around and leaned forward. "I found out something about Alice I thought you might want to know. Cole is beside himself."

I pulled my notebook and pen out. "Ready when you are."

She snatched the pen out of my hand. "Don't write it down," she hissed. "What if you lose your notebook?"

I took my pen back. "I never lose my notebook, but I won't write this one down since it's Alice."

"Her father is about to be charged with fraud."

My jaw dropped. "What?"

"Yes. I don't know the specific details. Everything is very hush-hush right now, but something like this doesn't happen all of a sudden. Alice has to know about it."

"It's possible she needs money," I mused.

"Yes. If you're still looking for a motive, she has a big one."

The server came over and took our drink order. When she left, I blew out a frustrated breath. "It fits, but I don't understand how they could have gotten a copy of his manuscript if he only sent it to his agent and editor."

"Data leak," Fletcher suggested. "Maybe he just doesn't realize it yet."

"He hasn't had any issues with his credit cards or anything of the sort. It's just this."

"Does he have good security?"

I nodded. "The best. He's paranoid about everything."

Fletcher snorted. "He has to be. Everyone is looking for a payday these days."

I scratched my head, my thoughts going in a million directions. "I still can't put Jane and Alice together, though. How do they know each other?"

"You said she was a writer?"

"Writer and one of Daniel's fans."

"The common denominator is Daniel. He's the link. You mentioned before he met Alice at a book signing?"

I nodded.

"Maybe he met Jane the same way?"

"It's possible. He claims to not know who she is, though."

"So you don't think he ever dated her?"

I groaned. "I hope not."

Fletcher laughed. "It's possible, and depending on how long ago it was, he may not even remember."

"She's far too young. Alice was on the precipice of being too young, but Jane would have been in college still when Daniel's last book was released."

Fletcher shrugged. "I've seen worse age differences."

At my look, she reached over and patted my hand. "It's hard when we get to know our friends a little too well, isn't it?"

"Ugh," I agreed. "I truly don't think he dated her, but the fact that I have to ask is creeping me out."

The server dropped off our drinks and left. When the first sip of sugary lemonade hit my soul, I sighed.

"Even if he didn't, he's still the link. You still don't know who's calling you both?"

"No, though I suspect it's Jane." I didn't want to say anything about Hardy coming over to work with me because it was far too early. We still had a lot to work out. But once he did, I would have access to a lot more cool toys and a better network of contacts. I couldn't ask him to trace a call. "Fletcher?"

She'd already sucked down half her iced tea.

"Do you know how I can have a call traced without getting the police involved?"

Her lips twisted. "Not officially. Was the number blocked?"

"Yes, and the voice was disguised."

"Depending on who your carrier is, the number might be unblocked on your phone records. I'd ask your carrier for a copy or see if you can download it from your account."

I had a lot to learn about being an official investigator. "Seriously?"

"It was a trick I learned a few years ago when I broke it off with a guy and he thought it would be cool to stalk me."

"Men," I muttered.

"Men," she agreed. "A friend of mine told me to check my phone records, and there it was clear as day."

Curious in spite of myself, I asked, "How did you get him to stop?"

A wicked smile curved Fletcher's lips. "I screenshotted a copy of those records and sent it to his mom."

I burst out laughing.

"She's a Kentucky mama. I bet she broke a switch off a tree and chased him down the highway with it."

We both cracked up. "I'll check," I said when I caught my breath. "That would be a lucky break."

"And one you need," she agreed. "If Alice needs money, I'd bet it's her squeezing him."

"I think you're right. She seemed awfully lovey-dovey when she was over there. If he won't be in a relationship with her, this would be the second-best thing."

I thought about something. "How rich is her family?" If her father was that big in the newspaper world, their fortune should be substantial.

Fletcher whistled low. "Mega rich. But I bet his assets

are tied up with the criminal case coming down the pipe. I can't speak for sure, but I know Alice has never held down a job in her life, and she's looking for a meal ticket once her dad gets locked up."

"If he does. He might have a lawyer clever enough to get him out of this."

Fletcher shrugged. "Good possibility, but it's going to take a long time." She dropped a few bills on the table and waved away my protests. "My treat. Keep what I told you to yourself, Dakota. You can't tell Daniel, and you especially can't tell Hardy."

I mimed zipping my lips.

"Figure it out soon, though. Cole got another call this morning. I don't think Daniel is going to get the full 48 hours."

Dread pooled in my stomach. "Got it. I'll do my best."

Fletcher grabbed her purse and slid out of the booth. "You're close. I can smell it."

I nodded my thanks and watched her hurry out the door.

I was close, but there were those few final missing pieces I needed to click into place before I could wrap things up.

TWENTY-THREE

I called Daniel on the way home.

"Everything okay?"

"Is this how everyone answers the phone when I call them these days?"

Daniel huffed. "I can honestly say I've never had to have a friend's car repaired for milk damage until I met you."

I burst out laughing. "She used milk?" My nose wrinkled. "Gross."

"Gross isn't even the half of it." I could almost see him rubbing that space between his eyebrows. "I have to suggest something to you, and you aren't going to like it."

"I haven't liked all that much of the last few months, so what's one more thing?"

He groaned. "I'm sorry, but Alice didn't only damage the interior. She popped your hood and poured it all over the engine and everywhere else she could think of."

I almost dropped my phone. "What?"

"I think they're going to total your vehicle."

"Daniel!"

"I was previously unaware of how...malicious Alice could be." The admission sounded begrudging.

"Don't you dare feel sorry for yourself when my car is in the shop full of rotting milk," I growled.

"I think it's a good thing you didn't report this to your insurance."

A disbelieving laugh escaped me. "I'm pretty sure they don't cover milk bandits."

"Is the vehicle I gave you working out?"

"It's fine," I snapped, annoyed at this entire situation. This disaster with Alice wasn't Daniel's fault, but it wasn't mine either, and now my car was ruined. "But a Beemer isn't exactly inconspicuous in this town. I have to be extremely careful when I'm tailing someone."

Daniel laughed. "I never thought I'd hear you say that sentence." He paused. "I'd like to reimburse you for the vehicle. You're welcome to keep the one I let you borrow, or I can write you a check for the MSRP so you can get a new one."

"You know that's not necessary." I had plenty of money. Not that I wanted my first purchase to be a new car I didn't total.

His voice softened. "I know you have plenty of money, but that's not the point. Your vehicle was damaged at my house. It's my responsibility."

I scoffed. "We both know that's not true. It's Alice's

fault. Though I'm curious why you aren't insisting she pay for the damages."

He fell silent. I waited until I realized he wasn't going to answer at all. My hands tightened around the steering wheel. "Daniel?"

"Alice has fallen on difficult financial times," he gritted out.

"Oh, my gosh," I breathed. "Even knowing what you already know, you gave her money?"

"Dakota..."

"Nope." How did he know about her father? Or did she give him some other sob story?

"Once this is over, I won't take another job from you." This was all too much. As much as I wanted to help my friends out, diving this deep into their personalities and personal business made me feel intrusive and, to be honest, a little gross. Some separation between friends and loved ones was a good thing. I certainly never expected to dive off the deep end right into Daniel Jensen's love life.

"Dakota—"

I hung up the phone and drove home steaming with anger.

My phone went off the second I stepped into the house.

She's here. I couldn't talk.

The message was from Daniel. I squeezed my eyes shut.

Why is she there?

She showed up and won't leave. She's hysterical on the floor.

Do you want me to send Hardy?

I remembered my promise to Fletcher. If Daniel didn't know about Alice's father, I couldn't tell him.

Will he come unofficially?

I'll ask.

I'm going to delete these messages. Just respond with a yes or no if he's coming, please.

Will do.

I called Hardy next and explained the situation. Instead of concern, he started laughing.

"Hardy!"

"This is a social media stunt waiting to happen. Is he sure he's not being recorded?"

I groaned. "I don't think he is, but there's no way to know. He's asking if you can go over unofficially and get her to leave."

"If you make that wonderful basil pasta for me, I will happily go over there and haul his errant ex-girlfriend out."

This time, I couldn't help laughing. "Of course I will. And thank you."

"Is there anything I should know?"

I told him everything except for the pending criminal charges.

"Interesting," he mused. "Have you told Daniel everything?"

"Nope," I said happily.

"Good. I'll head over in the next few minutes. He's

lucky I have an opening in my schedule. We still on for tonight?"

"Absolutely."

"Izzy is dying to meet you."

My heart warmed. "I'm nervous," I admitted. "But looking forward to it."

"She'll love you," Hardy said.

"I'll accept lukewarm if she needs more time."

"See you tonight."

We hung up, and I shot Daniel the text.

Yes.

Hurry, he responded.

An hour or so later, I received a message from Daniel with a picture of Hardy hauling Alice out of his house by the elbow.

A sharp crack of laughter escaped me.

Thanks.

I didn't do anything except call Hardy.

We should meet and talk.

Can't tonight. I have plans.

Be careful. Alice is acting increasingly erratic, and she seems to have a single-minded hatred toward you.

I'm the one with the milk car, I reminded him.

I reminded her of the same thing. Just promise you'll be careful.

I tore the metaphorical bandage off. *I'll be with Hardy.*

I see.

There wasn't anything left to say, so I ended with, *I'll be careful. I promise.*

I put my phone away and checked Poppy's bowl. She lay on her back in the middle of the living room rug, batting at an imaginary enemy.

"You good?" I called.

Poppy eyed me but didn't come running for the bowl, so I assumed she was good.

"I'm going out tonight. Don't destroy the house."

She meowed this time. "I'll be with Hardy," I said patiently.

Her meow this time was softer, making me chuckle. "I know you like him."

Poppy rolled to her feet and followed me to the bedroom. "Silly cat."

She hopped onto my bed while I flipped through my closet, searching for something to wear for ice cream. It was getting colder every day, but it was still early enough in the season to enjoy ice cream.

I should wear jeans and a sweater. It was sensible, warm, and comfortable.

But I was going out with Hardy for the first time in a long while. Too long. And I was meeting his daughter.

I pulled out a pair of leather leggings and an oversized tunic, then rummaged through the shoe rack until I found a pair of cute, low-heeled booties. Sensible, stylish, and warm.

Nailed it.

I left my hair down, curled the ends, and put on a little mascara, blush, and lip gloss. My stomach clenched with nerves.

"Calm down," I told myself. "She's a little girl, not a tiger."

I pressed a hand against my stomach and let out a slow breath. If I was this nervous now and hadn't even left my house, I couldn't imagine what I'd be like when I pulled into the parking lot. I sprayed the perfume I knew Hardy liked in the air and walked through it.

"Be good," I told Poppy and scratched behind her ears.

I grabbed my coat and purse and headed out the door.

HARDY AND IZZY sat at a small round table. He wore a pair of dark-wash blue jeans and a blue pullover that brought out the color of his eyes. Izzy wore a pair of blue fleece leggings and a black sweater with fuzzy boots.

She watched me with wide eyes as I came over to the table.

Hardy's eyes crinkled at the edges as he rose. "Dakota." He pressed a kiss against my cheek and took me by the hand.

"Izzy, this is Dakota."

I smiled. "Hello, Izzy."

She blinked at me with identical eyes to Hardy's. "Hello." Izzy smiled, displaying an adorable gap in her front teeth. "Are you Daddy's girlfriend?"

"Uh," I said eloquently.

"Yes," Hardy said firmly.

I snapped my attention to him. "Yes?"

His lips twitched. "Yes. Right?"

I jerked my head in a nod. "Yes. Right."

Izzy's eyes narrowed. "Are you sure?"

A laugh bubbled from me. "Yes. I'm sure."

"Okay," she said. "Can we get ice cream now?" Izzy hopped out of her seat and looked at her father expectantly.

"Go ahead and pick out what you want," he said.

Izzy skipped over to the counter. She was just tall enough to stand on her tiptoes and peek through the shield to see the flavors.

"Was it really that easy?" I whispered to him.

Hardy chuckled. "She's a pretty easygoing kid. It won't always be this way, but tonight I'm going to take the win."

"Alright then."

He held out his arm. "Ready for an ice cream coma?"

I hadn't had dinner yet, but I took his arm. "Always."

Izzy was six years old and had just started kindergarten. Her favorite subject was recess, and her favorite lunch was dino nuggets with apples. The gap in her teeth caused a lisp every time she spoke, and she'd managed to steal my heart less than half an hour after meeting her.

"What's your favorite color?" she asked, her lips and teeth blue from her cotton candy ice cream.

"Blue. Purple is in second place. What about you?"

"Pink. Yellow is in second place."

We smiled at each other.

"Do you have a dog?"

I shook my head. "I have a cat."

Izzy's eyes lit up. "What color?"

"Orange and white."

"Can I pet it?"

I laughed. "If it's okay with your dad."

She looked at Hardy, who laughed.

"Soon. I want you and Miss Dakota to get to know each other better before we go to each other's houses."

Izzy pouted. "Can she bring it next time we go for ice cream so I can pet it?"

"Her," I said. "My cat's name is Poppy, and she's a girl."

"Animals aren't allowed in stores," Hardy said.

Izzy frowned. "Why not?"

"Because some people might be allergic," he said.

"I'm not!" she boasted proudly.

"No, you're not, but Miss Dakota still can't bring the cat into the ice cream shop." He ruffled her hair and gave her a fond smile.

She gave him an adorable gap-toothed grin. "Got a picture?" she asked me.

I pulled my cell out and scrolled through my photo album. The real question was, how did I pick one picture out of the twelve hundred I currently had in my camera roll?

I showed her the one where Poppy lay on her back, glaring up at me with her chartreuse eyes.

Izzy gasped. "She's so cute!"

"She is. Sometimes she's grumpy, though."

Poppy tolerated the kids at the bookstore well. I'd never once seen her hiss or try to scratch any of them, but she had her limits. Once she met them, she'd slink away and hide until they all went away. Izzy was a well-behaved child, so far, so she and Poppy would probably be fine.

"Why is she grumpy?"

I laughed. "Because she's a cat. Most of them get grumpy for no reason."

"I used to have a dog," she said.

My eyes met Hardy's. "Oh?"

She nodded. "His name was Derby. He had spots."

"What color spots?"

"Black and white. Mom said he was like a Dalmatian but a mutt."

I smiled. "You liked your dog?"

She nodded. "But I don't get to see him anymore."

My heart cracked. I wasn't sure what to say without giving her false hope. Telling her she might get to see him soon felt cruel, because Hardy said her mom had no intentions of returning to Silverwood Hollow.

I couldn't imagine not coming back for my own flesh and blood, but I was doing my best to reserve judgment. It wasn't my place to speculate on her reasons or lack thereof. "I'm sorry to hear that."

Izzy nodded. "It's okay. Mom said he's having a lot of fun at the farm."

I blinked, horror widening my eyes.

Hardy choked. "A real farm, Dakota." He fumbled with his cell phone and pulled up a picture of an adorable black and white shepherd mix frolicking in a field with cows.

"Thank goodness," I said faintly, praying it wasn't Photoshopped.

Hardy's rumbling chuckle made me smile.

We finished up our ice cream, and I was having such a nice time, I didn't want to go home. But it was a school night, and I knew Hardy liked keeping her to a firm schedule.

We cleaned up our ice cream mess and walked out, Izzy skipping in front of us.

"She's adorable," I told him.

"I know," he said and smiled.

"How are you handling all of this?"

"Good days and bad. She's an entirely new human I had to meet and get to know. She likes her eggs a certain way and doesn't like when her sausage touches her syrup. If I get the generic honey oat cereal, she won't eat it. It has to be the name brand one. But if I get the generic fruity cereal, it's fine." He let out an exasperated sigh, tempering it with a patient smile. "I have to remember to ensure she's in bed by 8:30 and then remember she has to be up at seven for school."

Izzy bent down to touch a flower in a ceramic pot.

"It's a lot, but I've never been so fulfilled and challenged."

Tears filled my eyes as I squeezed his arm. "You're doing a wonderful job."

He put his hand over mine. "Thank you. I am so sorry it led to our split."

"No." I held my hand up. "It was a shock I felt wholly

unprepared for." I looked down at my feet. "To be honest, I'm still not prepared for it. I can't even imagine how you are."

His lips tilted into a wry smile. "No one is ever prepared for it."

A soft laugh escaped me. "I can see why. I'm not sure I could handle the challenge even a quarter as well as you have."

"I highly doubt that." Hardy called for Izzy, who skipped over to us. We walked to my car and stopped. "Want to say goodbye to Miss Dakota?"

I crouched down and held out my hand for a shake. To my surprise, she hurtled herself toward me. Stunned at her reaction, I caught her just as she threw her arms around my neck. I blinked away moisture and let her squeeze me. Enveloping her in a hug, I inhaled the scent of her strawberry shampoo and the cotton candy ice cream she'd dripped on her collar. Something inside of me melted.

I cleared my throat. "It was very nice to meet you, Izzy."

She held on for a long moment, and I let her. My mom always told me never to break a hug first because you never knew how much the other person needed it. The words came back to me, so I stayed crouched on the ground and let her hold on to me as long as she needed to.

A strange look passed over Hardy's face, his eyes flashing with regret, but he didn't intervene. When Izzy stepped back, her eyes were filled with tears.

I made no move to stand yet. "Are you okay?" I asked quietly.

She nodded and buried her face in the side of Hardy's thigh. Rising, I brushed a hand over her glossy hair and stepped back. It wasn't appropriate for me to kiss Hardy right now.

"Thank you both for the ice cream. I'm going to go home and try to make sure I didn't ruin my dinner with all the rocky road I ate."

I winked at Hardy and stepped off the curb toward my car.

He rested the back of his hand against his daughter's hair. "I'll see you soon." His blue eyes were warm as he watched me get inside my car. I waved and smiled at Izzy and drove away.

I was already in love with one of them, but it wouldn't be hard to fall in love with both in very different ways.

TWENTY-FOUR

Early the next morning, Hardy knocked on my door. Startled and still half asleep, I opened it and was about to ask him why he was here, when he pushed a steaming latte at me and brushed a kiss across my lips.

I accepted the drink and blinked up at him, speechless.

He gave me a wicked grin, shut the door behind him, and walked me back into the living room with one hand around my waist.

"Erm. Hi," I said once I shook off my surprise.

He kissed me again. I melted into him as Hardy took my drink and leaned over to set it on the coffee table.

I was breathless by the time he let go of me. "What in the world, Hardy?"

"I missed you," he said simply.

I sank onto the couch and reached for my drink. "Thank you."

He sat beside me. "You're welcome."

"How's Izzy?"

He smiled. "Wonderful. She's already asking when we can see Miss Dakota again." His expression sobered. "We have to be careful."

I pulled my legs up and laid them across his lap. "I know. I'd never do anything to hurt either of you."

"Are you sure you want to..." He waved his hand around. "Be with me. I'm a package deal now."

"I wouldn't have offered to meet her if I didn't want to." He'd bought me a London Fog latte. Mmm. "She's a wonderful child, Hardy. You're doing a great job with her." But something was weighing on my mind and had been since I'd gotten in my car last night. "I'm concerned about her mother."

His face hardened.

"Not about you and her. I've always trusted you in that regard. But with Izzy. Do you think she'll come back into her life?"

"We're finalizing things in court. She will have no parental rights soon."

I thought that was the way it was going, but he and I had never spoken about the details concerning his ex and daughter. I reached over and touched his arm. "For what it's worth, I'm very sorry. I don't understand this and perhaps never will. No child deserves something like this."

He lay his hand on top of mine. "I'm not sure what her goal was when she first came back. She said she wanted to be a family, but she abandoned Izzy when I wasn't interested in rekindling things. Maybe that was what she wanted all along. My decision just sped things along."

"It doesn't make any of this right."

"No." His jaw clenched. "I should have the documents in the next few months, and she has shown no interest in seeing Izzy."

"Poor Izzy," I murmured.

"When she hugged you—" Hardy cleared his throat. "It broke my heart."

"Mine too."

"We're really doing this?" he asked. There was a vulnerable note in his voice I rarely heard.

"As long as you haven't changed your mind."

He huffed. "I never changed my mind, Dakota."

"Even after everything happened, I still didn't want to live without you. I plan to make up for this, Hardy."

"You don't have to make up for anything. Your reaction was normal and warranted." He sipped his coffee. "I'm here for other things, though I'm glad we cleared this up."

"Other things? Like bringing me a latte?"

"Besides that. The police department has a consultant in for a few weeks training our IT department on cyber-crimes. I thought you might be interested in speaking with her."

I sat up a little straighter. "Yes! That would be amazing. I'm the least tech-savvy person I know, and this case has stumped me. The blackmailer has things they shouldn't have, and I believe Daniel when he says the only two people who had it wouldn't have released it. So they hacked him somehow. But they only took part of his manuscript." I frowned. "That's odd, right?"

"It's unusual, certainly. Normally, hackers are in it for a financial motive. Blackmail is less common, but it does occur. He'd do well to purchase a new computer and not hook it up to his Wi-Fi or any public internet until you get to the bottom of it."

"I hadn't thought of that, but it's a good idea. How soon can your consultant speak with me?"

"If you want to get ready, I'll drive you to the station."

I glanced down at my fox pajamas. "You think this is a little too casual?"

Hardy laughed. "I think it's adorable, but I'm not sure everyone else will."

"Can I finish my latte first?"

"Of course."

AN HOUR LATER, Hardy and I were on the road to the police station, even though I'd much rather still be in my fox pajamas lounging on the couch with him.

The Silverwood Hollow Police Department wasn't much to write home about; none of the government buildings in this town were, but they were functional.

Hardy walked me inside and led me all the way to the back of the building. A tall steel door loomed in front of us with a camera positioned toward the top left of the wall and a key card scanner by the door handle.

The camera flashed. Hardy waved at it and showed his

badge. There was a buzzing noise and a click, and the door opened, allowing us entrance.

"Super secret squirrel," I murmured under my breath.

"These are the cases they don't want anyone else to know about," Hardy said. "They release the minimum required by law and keep the rest hush hush until they're solved."

"I guess cybercrimes happen a lot around here?"

Hardy shrugged as we walked. "They're rampant everywhere, and rapidly advancing technology doesn't help."

He knocked on a blue door. "Cavanaugh," he said.

The door opened, revealing a pair of lively hazel eyes. "Detective." She held open the door and motioned us in. "You must be Dakota."

"Hello."

"I'm Kai." She held out a hand, and we shook. "Cavanaugh says you're working on a case where hacking might be involved?"

"Yes. Someone managed to take something from my client's laptop without his permission or awareness. He swears he only sent it to two trustworthy people."

Kai's tongue clicked. She was short, dark-haired, and olive-skinned. An intricate tattoo crawled from her wrist all the way up her arm until it disappeared into her sleeve. She was slim and dressed in olive-green slacks, nude flats, and a cream-colored blouse.

"It could have been anyone," she mused. "Has anyone visited his house lately? Any parties or social gatherings?"

"One a couple of months ago, but the troubles started after that. I wouldn't think any of those guests were responsible. They're all filthy rich."

"If they're trying to blackmail him, it doesn't matter if they're rich." She softened the words with a smile. "That's how power moves, Dakota. People are constantly looking for ways to move up in the world, and blackmail is the easiest way." She pulled a couple of chairs out for us. "Please. Have a seat."

Hardy scooted a little closer to me. Kai sat down in front of a computer, her fingers flying as she typed. "Sorry. Let me shoot this off really quick, and we can get to the nitty-gritty."

We waited while she took a few moments to finish up her task, and I looked around the room. There wasn't much to it. The back wall was filled with computers, dotted with random lights blinking in colored patterns. One long table lined the side of the wall, filled with electronic components I didn't recognize. Kai's desk was small and held one monitor, a hard drive, and a coffee cup filled with pens and pencils.

A lack of pictures or personal items displayed anywhere made the place feel sterile.

"I can run through the most common scams with you," Kai said as she turned back toward us, "but if there's anything specific you want to talk about, I'm happy to do so."

"And everything we say stays between us?"

Kai tilted her head in curiosity. "It will, unless I can make an interesting case study out of it."

"Minus the names?"

She grinned. "Minus the names."

"Good. Here's what I have." I bent down and pulled Daniel's file out, along with my notebook. "This is my first case, and I'm afraid I'm not as skilled as I would like in cyber cases. Someone is blackmailing him and threatening to derail his career, and I think they have a good chance at it if I can't figure out how to link these things together."

Kai's eyebrows rose as she slid everything over. "Let's go through it together, then."

"If you have time. I'm very appreciative of your help." Hardy deserved a home-cooked dinner for introducing me to her.

Kai smiled. "I always have time for intrigue."

TWENTY-FIVE

I walked out of Kai's office with a head full of new ideas and a brand-new disgust for humanity. The stories she told me saddened and sickened me, and most of them were only about money.

After this, I planned to sit Gran and Mom down and educate them thoroughly on how people make it their life's work bilking elderly people out of their life savings.

I barely answered my phone on a good day, so I'd be a difficult one to scam, but Gran would talk to a stone in the middle of the road if she thought it might talk back to her.

Neither of them was stupid, but they didn't have to be. Scams today were growing ever more sophisticated, and with voice cloning...

Don't even get me started about voice cloning.

When we were back on the road, I turned to Hardy. "Did you know about all that stuff Kai was talking about?"

He shook his head. "No. It makes me never want to click on a link ever again, though."

"Right?" I chuckled. "We're living in weird times, aren't we?"

"You can say that again." He laughed. "And I'm a lot more vulnerable than you because how many times have you called me saying you're in trouble?"

A belly-laugh escaped me. "Just ask the voice how we met before you do anything."

"Yes, Dakota. That's exactly what I'm going to do when I suspect you're about to be murdered." He sighed and shook his head, but it was more of an exasperated motion than an annoyed one.

"A code word then."

His brows flicked up. "Oh, yeah? Like potato?"

"Exactly like potato. But maybe not that one. A word we'd never use in normal conversation."

"I like that idea. What are you thinking?"

"Hushpuppy?"

Hardy lifted a shoulder in a shrug. "I like hushpuppies, and one day I might want them for dinner."

I eyed him. "Weird, but okay."

"What about lightsaber?" Hardy asked.

I groaned. "Nothing with that movie, please."

He laughed. "Your turn."

"Parthenon?"

"What if we're playing trivia?"

"Hardy! Have we ever played trivia together?"

"One day we might."

I laughed and swatted his shoulder. "Take this seriously. What about dahlia?"

His expression turned thoughtful. "Like the flower or the murder?"

My mouth opened and snapped shut. "What?"

"So the flower then," he murmured.

"The flower, yes. I've never used that word in a sentence that I can ever remember, and it's not common in the shops."

"I like it. Dahlia then. With all its forms. Plural and singular, with adjectives before and after."

"You're taking this way more seriously than I expected you to."

"Well," Hardy said mildly. "It's not every day you find out robots are cloning our voices and trying to steal all our money."

"Yes," I said faintly. "How about that?"

"It's settled then. Dahlia is our code word. If we use it once, we have to change it in case someone nefarious overhears it."

I snorted. "Of course. We wouldn't want a nefarious villain using it against us in the future."

He grinned and pulled into my driveway. "I have to get back to work."

"Thanks for introducing me." I started to ask him if he wanted to come for dinner, but things were different now.

His face softened, as if he knew what I was about to ask. "Don't overthink this. We've already been together for a while. Yes, we have to do some things differently, but Izzy likes you, and she's happy to spend as much time together as you want. If you're in this with me for the long haul, I am too."

A lump formed in my throat. "I am," I croaked. "Dinner tonight?"

"Here?"

I nodded.

"I'll ask Izzy. Mind eating a little earlier so I can get her back home for our nightly ritual?"

"Of course I don't mind."

"Plan on it, but I'll let you know for sure once I get her from school."

I kissed him and slid out of the car, waving as he drove away.

It wasn't yet lunchtime, so I called Daniel and asked him if I could drop by.

He sounded demoralized but told me to stop by. I didn't ask questions, figuring I could talk to him when I was there.

The gate opened, and I spotted only his car in the driveway. Relieved Alice hadn't shown up, I got out with the two bags of takeout I'd picked up on the way and knocked on his door.

Daniel opened it, his appearance sending me back a step. "Are you okay?" I blurted, as he held the door open.

"Let's eat outside," was all he said as he took the bags from me. "Mind leaving your phone in the house?"

I frowned but agreed. Whatever was going on seemed

serious. "I can't leave it for too long. Harper is at the shop by herself. We haven't hired anyone new yet."

"It won't take long."

A few minutes later, we were set up at one of the picnic tables at the back of the main house.

Daniel looked like he hadn't slept in days. His t-shirt was wrinkled, and he wore joggers, something I'd never seen him in. He had a five o'clock shadow dotting his cheeks and chin, and there were dark circles under his eyes.

He said nothing for a few minutes, inhaling his food like a starving man.

I watched him warily, giving him the space and time he needed to collect his thoughts.

When he spoke, I was entirely unprepared to hear what he had to say.

"She's watching me," he croaked.

I stopped cutting my food. "Excuse me?"

"She's been watching me. I don't know for how long."

"Who?" I demanded, though I suspected I knew.

"Alice."

"How?"

"Cameras inside the house. She replaced my plugs with the ones that have the cameras inside them."

I gawked at him. "Every plug?" I squeaked.

"No. Living room, office, and library. Places I do most of my business in."

My brow furrowed. "I don't understand. Why would she do that?"

"She wasn't interested in watching me, I don't think. Alice wanted to know the state of my financial affairs." His gaze flicked to me. "And if I was dating anyone."

"How did you find out?"

"One of the plugs shorted out." He snorted. "That's what she gets for cheaping out on equipment. I hired an electrician, and he showed the thing to me and asked if I knew it had a camera." Daniel sighed and shook his head. "I asked him to sweep my entire house."

"How in the world could a camera fit into a plug?"

"Not even the plug. A fake screw." Daniel scrubbed a hand over his face. "I've been safe for too long. It was bound to happen."

"No. That's not—no one deserves to have their privacy invaded. This was in no way your fault."

He stabbed at the pasta I bought him.

"When did she have time to install those?"

"She stayed the night here, and I left for a little while. She either did it herself or brought someone in."

"Does she know you know?"

"She will if she's looked at the camera footage."

I hadn't thought about that. "But you didn't contact her?"

"No. I never plan to speak to her again."

"When you dated before, did she ever stay over here?"

"All the time." He shook his head. "I know what you're thinking, but she isn't the one who stole my manuscript. I am overly paranoid about my work. My laptop never remained open. All my devices have passwords on them, and I don't leave anything in the Cloud or where it can be accessed or hacked. I write a lot on my hard drive and save it to separate storage."

"You aren't afraid of losing things?"

He laughed, but it was borderline hysterical. "Never lost a single thing until someone managed to snag my manuscript right out from under my nose."

"There's absolutely no way Alice could have gotten to it?"

"None. Unless she somehow guessed my password, which should be impossible. I don't write them down. Ever."

"And when she stayed this last time?"

"Even more paranoid," he assured me. "Alice is a terrible person, but she isn't the one who stole my work."

I chewed my chicken, thinking about his words. "Usually, the most obvious answer is the answer."

"Not this time. It's someone else. It has to be. Alice might have helped, but she wasn't the one who swiped it."

"Then it's Jane. I'm almost positive they're working together. Her vehicle was at Jane's house."

My fork clattered to my plate. She worked in IT. "Daniel," I said urgently. "Have you had any work done inside your house over the last few months?"

"Work? Like remodeling?"

I nodded.

"Not that I remember. The only person in the house for the last few months was the electrician I just hired."

I blew out a breath. "There goes that theory," I

muttered. If Jane had accessed his house, then that would link everything together.

"We're out here because you think she's still monitoring you?" I asked.

"I can't be too sure. The electrician found the ones in the plugs but told me he wasn't qualified to search for the rest." A thin smile pulled at his lips. "He suggested I contact the authorities."

"Maybe you should."

"Not yet. I feel like we're close to the end. I want to know why and who, and I don't want the authorities going through all my things before I mentally prepare myself."

"I can ask Hardy," I said quietly. "He could sweep your house and clear it of any listening devices."

His chest rose, and he exhaled a defeated breath. "Are you two officially back together?"

I nodded.

His eyes shut for a brief moment. "I expected it would happen. After our party and the way he looked at you—the way he looks at you every time you're in the same room." Daniel shook his head. "He is deeply in love with you, Dakota."

My cheeks flushed with color.

"Best of luck to you both. You know how I feel." He chuckled ruefully. "Though I must admit, I did not expect you to find my life and my past so...muddy."

I choked on a laugh.

His lips curved up into a smile. "If my life were an object right now, it would be a giant red flag."

Laughter bubbled up, and soon, I couldn't hold it in.

To his credit, Daniel laughed too. "What a mess," he muttered. "Moving forward, I'm going to run thorough background checks on everyone I date."

"Good luck. On paper, Alice appears perfect. She's beautiful, rich, all the things most men want."

Daniel shook his head. "Some like nosy small town bookstore owners."

I blushed. "Nosy is rude." I sniffed. "I prefer curious."

"Ah yes. *Curious*. That's what you are. More curious than you should be sometimes, though I asked you to do this, and I should have expected no less than you upending every stone in my garden."

"I'll have more answers for you soon. I promise."

"I know. Now, come. Let's finish our lunch and move to lighter topics."

"Sounds wonderful to me."

TWENTY-SIX

I forgot to ask Hardy if Izzy liked pasta. She was a kid. Didn't they all like pasta?

It was too late to ask. They'd be here in fifteen minutes. Maybe I had mac and cheese in the pantry. Should I—a knock on the door sounded.

They were early! Maybe I should have ordered a pizza.

I wiped my hands off on the towel and hurried to answer the door. Hardy and Izzy stood on the porch.

"Hi, Miss Dakota!" Izzy said and marched right into my house like she owned it. She looked adorable tonight in a pair of jeans and a white fuzzy sweater. A backpack bounced on her back as she walked in.

Hardy laughed. "Izzy!"

She turned to her dad. "What?"

"We're supposed to wait for Dakota to invite us in."

"We came all the way over here and she opened the door."

Kid logic. "She's not wrong," I said and laughed when Hardy rolled his eyes and stepped inside. He held a bottle of wine out to me.

"My favorite. Thank you!"

"You're welcome. It was the least I could do if you're cooking for us."

"You two have a seat. Izzy, would you like something to drink?"

"Do you have chocolate milk?"

I laughed. "I have the stuff to make it. Would you like a glass?"

She looked at her dad. Hardy nodded. "Yes, please!"

"Hardy? A glass of wine?"

"Not tonight. Water is perfect."

Izzy's high-pitched, "*Eeeeee, kitty!*" shriek almost made me drop the gallon of milk. Poppy had deigned to come out of her hiding spot in the bedroom. She sat in the middle of the living room staring up at Izzy with unblinking eyes.

"Can I pet her?" Izzy's voice sounded a little unhinged. Kids could not contain themselves when they saw adorable animals.

"Poppy?" I asked her. "What do you say?"

Poppy ran over to Izzy and wove between her ankles.

"I'd say that's a yes."

Izzy sat on her haunches and slathered attention on my cat while I fixed their drinks. It was a few minutes before Poppy walked away and headed back into the bedroom, having enough attention for one evening.

Izzy shrugged and came back into the kitchen, her eyes

lighting up when she saw the big glass of chocolate milk I gave her.

Hardy mouthed, *"smaller next time,"* and pinched his thumb and index finger together.

I winced. "Sorry."

I watched as Izzy sipped on her milk. "Do you like pasta?"

She tilted her head and thought about it. "What kind?"

"Mmm, Alfredo." It wasn't exactly an Alfredo. Close enough.

Izzy frowned. "I don't know what that is."

Hardy smiled and nodded. "She does."

"Dinner is almost finished. Maybe fifteen minutes?"

Hardy reached into Izzy's backpack and pulled out a container of map pencils and a coloring book. He didn't have to say a word. Izzy took everything and started coloring without a word, her little face screwed up in concentration.

She was adorable.

As I cooked, Hardy and I talked about safe subjects. No work or crime or any of the normal subjects we discussed.

I found out Izzy loved watching cartoons and playing board games, Hardy had never seen half of the eighties movies I loved, and his favorite candy bar was Mounds, which was an almost breakupable offense.

I confessed to loving old band t-shirts and still had some from my youth I couldn't bear to get rid of and possessing multiple copies of *The Old Man and The Sea.*

All in all, we spent a wonderful evening together. As afraid as I was about meeting Izzy, she'd quickly managed to charm me. She was bright, adorable, well-behaved, and friendly. I had to hand it to Hardy. He was doing a wonderful job with her.

I wondered again about the girl's mother, but it was a sore subject and one that wasn't really any of my business. I'd pried enough, so I left it alone and enjoyed the evening.

When it was time to go, Izzy cleaned up her map pencils and coloring books, tucking them back into her backpack. Poppy came out one more time to see what the commotion was all about and, much to Izzy's delight, jumped into her lap when Izzy called her over.

"Poppy is putting on a show tonight," Hardy murmured in my ear.

"Izzy is a likable kid. Plus, she hasn't pulled on her tail or ears even once. The kids in the bookstore give her a run for her money sometimes."

"She's gentle with animals from what I've seen so far. Poppy might have a friend for life."

He slung her backpack over his shoulder and gave her a few minutes to love on the cat before he called her over.

"Aww," Izzy whined.

I hid my smile behind my hand.

"It's a school night, and you still need a bath."

"You'll see her again very soon," I promised. Poppy hopped off her lap and turned to face Izzy.

"You're so cute," Izzy gushed. With a sigh, she rose and dragged her feet over to Hardy.

"Come on, kiddo," he said with a laugh. "Dakota is right. You'll be back over here soon enough."

Her face brightened at that, but Izzy turned and gave Poppy a sorrowful look before following her dad out the door.

"Thanks for dinner," Hardy said once he had Izzy buckled up and secured. "I meant what I said. If you'll have us, we'll be back as much as you want us."

I touched Hardy's face. "We've been through enough. It's early days with her, I know, but when the time is right..." I paused as my heartbeat kicked up several notches. "Maybe soon you won't have to leave at all."

Hardy's gaze locked onto my face. "That would be one of the greatest things that ever happened to me." His eyes softened. "To us," he amended. "Early days," he agreed. "But I hope soon."

"She's going through a tough time with her mom and the adjustment. We have all the time in the world."

Hardy brought me in for a hug and kissed the top of my head. "Next weekend. Friday night? Me and you?"

I nodded against his chest. "Yes."

"Good." He stepped away. "I'll call you tomorrow."

Hardy drove away. Izzy waved to me the entire time until they turned onto the road and became a speck in the distance.

As soon as I walked back into the house, my phone dinged with a message from Cole.

I'm so sorry. I had to.

TWENTY-SEVEN

Cole refused to answer the phone and wouldn't respond to any texts.

If you don't answer, I'm going to come over!

When he still didn't answer, I rang Fletcher.

"I just heard. He's avoiding you, isn't he?"

"What is he talking about?"

Fletcher sighed. "Let me guess. He sent you a cryptic text, then went radio silent?"

"Yep."

"The caller told him they would release the proof tomorrow."

I sank onto the couch. "Cole did the story, didn't he?"

"I'm afraid so."

Tears sprang to my eyes. "Did he give Daniel a heads up?"

"Highly unlikely." Fletcher's voice softened. "He's not friends with Daniel Jensen. This is just a story to him. A career maker. I just saw the proof of tomorrow's paper."

"But it won't only be this paper, will it?"

"I'm afraid not. Jensen has a massive following. All the major news outlets will pick the story up."

I groaned and slumped against the cushions. "I need to call Daniel."

"It won't stop this. I'm sorry."

"He should at least be prepared." I chewed on the side of my thumbnail. "And there's absolutely nothing I can do?"

Fletcher sighed. "If by some miracle you solve the case by tomorrow before seven a.m., we can retract the story. Everything is digital these days, so it won't be as complicated as it used to be, but we have a small print run going out, and we can't change those. They're already being printed."

"So either way, it has the chance of blowing up."

"I'm afraid so."

"There's not much I can do tonight, anyway. It's after nine." I could go by Alice's house and Jane's and see if they were together, but I wasn't sure what good it would do me. But the first thing I should do is stop by Daniel's house. News like this shouldn't be given over text.

"Do you know where Cole is?" I asked.

"Hiding from you, I'm sure," Fletcher said, an amused note in her voice.

"I take it you haven't seen him?"

"Not since this afternoon. He came in after lunch and

had the door shut the rest of the day. Whatever it was he was working on seemed important."

"Obviously," I growled.

"We haven't known each other long, but you seem like someone a friend can count on. Once you solve this, we'll clear things up with a new story. It's a small town, Dakota. We're not in the business of ruining lives if we don't have to."

"That's not as comforting as you think it is," I said.

"Yes, well, I'm afraid Daniel Jensen might have a very bad day tomorrow, and there's nothing I can do about it."

"Thanks for chatting. I'm going to run to Daniel's house."

"Anytime. I'll text you if I see your errant reporter."

We hung up, and I ran into my bedroom to switch out my sandals for boots and my blouse for a warm sweater.

When I was suitably cozy, I hurried out the door to catch Daniel before he went to bed.

Daniel's eyes widened when he saw me on his doorstep.

"Dakota? What's wrong?"

"We might need to talk in the yard," I said, untangling my scarf from around my neck as I stepped into his house.

"Of course." He eyed my attire. "Do you want a heavier jacket?"

"If you have one. I was in a hurry today."

He held up a finger and walked away. I leaned against the wall, trying to slow my racing heart. When he returned, he held up a fleece-lined trench coat.

"Thanks."

He'd taken the time to shrug on a jacket over his lounge pants and t-shirt. "Gloves?"

"I'm okay for now."

"Alright then, let's head out. You're making me extremely nervous this evening."

"Sorry. I thought you'd want to hear this in person and not via text."

"Even more curious."

He led me to the same picnic tables as the other day. We sat across from each other, and he crossed his fingers.

"Must be bad news," he said mildly. "I've never seen you struggle for words."

"The Gazette is running a story on you tomorrow," I blurted.

Shock widened his eyes. He jerked back as if I'd struck him. "What?"

"Your blackmailer has been in touch with one of the reporters there and offered him the story, but only for a limited time. I received a tip this evening that the story would run first thing in the morning."

Daniel scrubbed a hand over his chin. "And there's nothing we can do to stop it?"

"Solve the case." A hysterical laugh bubbled from me. "Something I've been trying to do from the moment you gave it to me."

A door creaked open from one of the small cabins he had dotted around his property.

"Mr. Jensen?" a woman called. She walked over to us.

I recognized her from the party Daniel had thrown me a while ago. "Hello," I said and smiled at her.

"Ah! Miss Adair. How nice to see you again."

She turned her attention to Daniel. "Would you like some refreshments?"

"No, thank you," he said. "We didn't mean to disturb you this evening. Dakota and I are chatting, but she won't be here long."

"Ma'am," I said before she could walk away. "Do you mind if I ask a question?"

The woman looked at Daniel who merely shrugged.

"Did you ever have anyone over to look at anything in the house, specifically for the internet or Wi-Fi?"

Daniel sighed. "Dakota, I told you—"

"We did," the woman said.

Daniel's mouth snapped shut. "Martina. You did?"

"Yes, sir. It was when you went to visit your editor. We were out of the internet for almost a full twenty-four hours, so we called the provider. They sent a woman over that same day."

Daniel and I locked gazes.

"Was her name Jane?"

Her eyes narrowed. "It sounds familiar, but it was a while ago."

I fished for my cell phone and searched Jane's name and our town. A picture of Jane pulled up, and I handed the phone to the woman. "Does she look familiar?"

Martina frowned down at it. "Oh. Yes. That's her."

"Was she ever in Daniel's office?"

She nodded.

"And did she access any of his computers?"

She nodded again. "I don't have any of his passwords, but she told me I didn't need to worry about it."

Daniel wore a stunned expression. "That's how she did it."

"It would seem so."

"Did I do something wrong?" Martina asked.

"Not at all. Please don't worry," Daniel assured her. "Was Alice here during that time?"

Martina frowned before nodding. "Yes, sir."

Daniel muttered something under his breath and let out a long sigh. "Thank you. Please enjoy the rest of your evening."

Martina turned and walked away, her face stricken.

"You're going to have to talk to her tomorrow. She looks devastated," I whispered.

"It wasn't her fault. It was mine."

"It was Alice and Jane's fault. That's all. You can't blame yourself for their actions."

Daniel groaned and rubbed his hands over his face. "Here I thought I was being so careful and clever. I was always so paranoid about things, and those two waltzed right in and ruined my life!"

"Not ruined," I said. "We will fix this. Even if the story breaks tomorrow, once we catch them, you will be the wronged party."

"It's about perception. If this story breaks, it's going to be difficult to come back from."

I sat up a little straighter. "Do you have surveillance in your house?"

Daniel blinked. "I do."

We both rose at the same time.

"Race you," he said.

I laughed for the first time in a while and took off like a rocket.

Daniel beat me, of course, because he had several inches on me and wore a less heavy coat, but I didn't care. We finally had something. If we could show them colluding, and if I could piece together how they knew each other, I'd have this case in the bag.

Daniel led me into the library and fired up his PC.

"Does Alice know about these?"

His brow furrowed for a moment. "I don't believe I've ever mentioned them. If I had, I think Alice would have tried to access that footage instead of installing her own, wouldn't she?"

"I agree. This is good. Go back to when you left for that meeting."

Daniel flipped through the files.

"Do you have a laptop I can use so I don't have to do this on my phone?"

He reached into a drawer and pulled out a shiny iPad. "Will this do?"

"Perfect. You search for the footage, and I'll do some more digging on Jane. Do you have a list of all your signings going back a year?"

"They should still be on my website."

Now we were cooking. "Tell me when you have something." I snapped my fingers. "If you have footage from that day, it should include when she installed those cameras and who was with her."

"Let's hope."

We fell silent as we worked. It took me quite a while to find anything about Jane other than where she worked. I had a gut feeling I knew where Alice and Jane had met, but it took some digging. Daniel had traveled all over the place during the last twelve months. I decided to go back six months, so I had to cross-reference his website for the date and location, then access the bookstore's website and social media and hope they'd taken pictures of the event.

I hit pay dirt four months back. "Got you," I murmured.

Daniel sucked in a breath. "They met?"

I turned the iPad around. Jane and Alice sat together in the audience at one of his signings. He swore under his breath.

"Is that about how long you've known Alice?"

"Roundabout," he agreed. "I've been such a fool."

"Did you know Alice's father was about to be brought up on criminal charges?"

He blinked in surprise. "No," he said slowly. "She never mentioned it."

"The financial difficulties were something else?" I probed.

"She said her father wanted her to accept more responsibility, and she couldn't access her trust for another year.

Alice swore she'd pay me back." His laugh had a strangled sound to it. "This is what it was. Her piggy bank was drying up, and she thought she could use me to replenish it."

"Sure seems like it."

There was one thing I had forgotten to do. Something that might tie this all together. "Let me check one more thing." I logged into my phone records for the bookstore and scrolled down to the day and time I'd received the call.

None of the numbers were blocked. "Jackpot," I whispered. "Do you have Alice's cell number?"

Daniel rattled the first six numbers off.

Bingo.

"I think we have them," I said. My fingers shook as I turned the device around to show him.

"That's Alice's number!" he exclaimed. "This was the person who called you to try to force you to cancel my book signing?"

"It was."

"Why is her number not showing up as blocked on your records?"

I shrugged. "It was a tip I got from Fletcher. She said sometimes they don't show up as blocked when it's on the records because they only blocked the number from the other phone and not the network. Or something like that. We got lucky with this one."

"I'll say."

Daniel froze as he clicked through the video he had pulled up on his screen. "There you are," he whispered.

I scrambled to my feet, the iPad forgotten, and watched over his shoulder.

Alice answered Daniel's door, letting Jane, holding a black duffle, inside. We watched as they went into the kitchen and Jane removed several small boxes from the bag.

"The cameras," Daniel said.

I let out a low whistle as I watched Jane unbox them. I'd never realize someone was watching me with one of those because I had no idea cameras could come in that small of a package.

"Your cameras are really good."

"State-of-the art. One can never be too careful."

We both cracked a laugh at that one.

"If I check them on a regular basis," Daniel said dryly. "I'd all but forgotten they were here to be honest. I've had them for so long and the only people in the house are the staff I occasionally keep and you." He shook his head. "Sloppy of me."

"It's your private space. I wouldn't have thought to do it either."

"Nor did I think Alice was responsible. I guess money can drive people to insane lengths."

"How much was she trying to get out of you?"

"Three million."

I choked. "*What?*"

"My career is worth far more, but yes, that would have put a dent in my life for sure."

"Geez," I whispered.

We continued watching as Jane installed the plugs, then watched as she showed Alice how to access the feed. As we watched, something else clicked. That thread with the *itgirl2000* didn't mean *it* girl. It meant I.T. girl. The messages on that board had to be from Jane.

"She has to know by now you've found them," I observed.

"More than likely."

"I'm going to text Hardy. He has his daughter tonight, but he should be able to send out another officer."

"What if we waited?" Daniel asked.

I lowered my phone. "For what?"

"What if we confronted them?"

"Do you really want to do that?" I asked. "I'll at least contact Cole and Fletcher and send them evidence to withdraw the story."

Daniel's shoulders slumped. "Thank you."

"He'll get a two for one. The story about Alice's father is about to break, and he'll get to write about Alice, too." I frowned. "Well. Only if she's arrested." I laid a hand on his shoulder. "I've always been caught up in confronting people, and it always turns out dangerous for me and the people I care about." I thought of Hardy and Izzy. "How about we just turn this in to the police this time and let them handle it?"

He looked up at me with a knowing stare. "Things are changing for you, aren't they?"

"Things and me. I never thought being in danger was fun, but there was an element of excitement that kept it interesting. But the last case..." I sighed. "I want to know I'm going to wake up each day. It doesn't mean I'll always manage to stay out of the line of fire, but I can be a lot more careful than I was before to prevent it."

His smile crinkled the edges of his eyes. "I never thought I'd see Dakota Adair be the voice of reason when it came to an investigation."

I laughed and swatted him on the shoulder. "Make copies of that. Email them to me and send them to yourself, too. Do you have the surveillance from a few months ago?"

Daniel leaned forward and clicked through several folders. "Just in time," he murmured. "It wipes every six months."

"I can't imagine how much storage you have to keep that much video."

"It's saved me three million, hasn't it?"

I laughed. "Sure did."

Before he went through those folders, he emailed me the videos from the plug-in camera installation, so I texted Hardy, warning him about what happened and asked where I should send the video.

You caught them in the act?

Daniel's fancy surveillance he forgot about did.

Oh, to be rich.

I did not remind him that, technically, I was rich, too. Soon, I wanted to sit down with him and talk about things. When things were settled, and we were both 100% sure this was it for us. We could do so many things with the money, and Izzy would never want for anything.

I put a hand over my stomach and let out a slow breath. A few months ago, I was flipping out about the possibility of having a kid. Now, I was thinking about the potential colleges she could go to loan-free.

Oh, how times had changed.

Slow down, I told myself.

Can you believe he didn't think to check?

I can. I'm with Izzy, so I can send a car over, or you can email me what you have, and we can take care of it first thing.

I relayed the info to Daniel. "Would you rather Hardy oversee this personally? If so, I can email him everything, and he'll get on it first thing."

"I'm more worried about the news story, so tomorrow morning is fine."

I'll email you.

See you tomorrow.

I messaged Cole and said the one thing I've always wanted to say.

STOP THE PRESSES.

TWENTY-EIGHT

Hardy stopped by first thing the next morning.

"Thought you might want to ride a long while we pick up Jane and Alice."

I tilted my head and studied him. "Who are you, and what have you done with Detective Cavanaugh?"

He laughed and snagged me around the waist. "I spoke with Daniel this morning, and he made a point of telling me you chose to sit this one out to keep yourself safe." Hardy pressed a kiss to the side of my neck, sending gooseflesh rising all over my body. "So I thought I'd come here and reward you." He pressed another kiss to my throat.

"Well," I said breathlessly, "perhaps I should use caution in all my endeavors then. Who knows what I'll be rewarded with?"

Hardy laughed against my neck. "Who knows, indeed?"

"Can Poppy come?"

He shrugged. "Why not? Let's see what Poppy has to think about everything."

I poured him a cup of coffee. "Let me change and throw my hair up, and I'll be ready."

Hardy waved me away and reached for the coffee.

Fifteen minutes later, I had Poppy and my bag, and we were ready to go.

Hardy grabbed the hammock from my car and hung it in his so Poppy would feel more relaxed.

"It's weird that your cat likes this stuff."

I glanced back at the orange Persian staring at him and laughed. "She is oddly intuitive with investigations, but she's been unusually quiet for this one."

"Maybe you didn't need help," Hardy suggested.

"I always need help," I said with a laugh.

Hardy reached for the portable radio and said something I didn't quite understand, but I assumed he was telling the others he was en route.

"Alice first?" I said.

"She's the one most likely and able to flee."

"Maybe not for long. Fletcher said her father was about to be charged with fraud."

Hardy's eyebrows rose. "Really?" He whistled. "I'm not surprised. There have been rumors for years."

"Alice saw a jackpot with Daniel. She must have known which way the wind was blowing for a while now."

"Cole canceled the story?"

I nodded. "Begrudgingly. He was marginally better when I told him about Alice and Jane, so don't be surprised if he conveniently shows up when you serve the warrant."

Hardy's jaw tightened. "I can't stand reporters, but Cole isn't as bad as some."

"Fletcher seems like one of the good ones, too. Maybe even better than Cole."

Hardy glanced at me. "Good. You need female friends."

My jaw dropped. "Hardy!"

"I'm serious," he said with a chuckle. "I thought Trudy was heading that way..." His voice trailed off.

"Yeah," I said softly. "Me too."

"Plus, Daniel is going to do his best to steal you away from me, so your chess nights will now be supervised."

I bit down my protests because he probably wasn't wrong. "I can handle myself," I said primly.

"Yes, we both know you can. But you and I are endgame, Dakota."

I sucked in a breath.

"I—"

"Aren't we?"

Tears filled my eyes. "We are," I concurred. "I've been thinking about some things, and I want to talk to you about that money."

"That money requires a prenuptial agreement," Hardy growled.

"Prenup," I said faintly.

Hardy barked a laugh and put his hand over mine. "Eventually. Please don't pass out."

"I guess I never thought about any kind of formalized agreement if I got married, but it's a wise move."

"I don't want you to think I'm with you for it. I've never told a soul."

"I don't. But I want to do some things. With you and for Izzy."

His brow furrowed. "Izzy?"

"Like college. Maybe a house much later. We can put money away for her, so she won't have to struggle when she graduates."

Hardy pulled over on the side of the road and unbuckled his seat belt.

"Hardy? Are you o—?"

His lips swept over mine, claiming them in a burning kiss that left me breathless. When he pulled away, all I could do was blink at him in surprise.

"You are the best thing that's ever happened to me," he growled. "I've already set up a college fund for Izzy, and we can talk about the other things later. We have plenty of time. The most important thing here is that you're including my daughter in these things, and for that, I've never been more grateful."

"Package deal," I said faintly.

He grinned and pulled away, clicking his seat belt closed. "Package deal," he agreed.

Hardy pulled into the same parking lot I used when I followed Alice. We watched the house for a while until he radioed the others and told them to move in.

Her red Mustang was parked in the front drive, and

there was no movement in the house. It was still early morning, so she might still be asleep.

I grimaced. The next several minutes would not be a great way to wake up, but that was what you got when you committed multiple felonies.

Poppy, sensing something was up, had popped her head up and was staring out the window, oddly looking right at Alice's house.

Hardy pulled out of the lot and was the first into the driveway.

"Stay here. Don't get out until we have Alice cuffed, okay?"

"Was it okay bringing me here?"

He flashed me a smile. "I'm a short timer now. I don't really care."

I grinned at him. "Twice today you've managed to surprise me."

Hardy winked and grabbed a small file from his dash before heading up the steps to knock on Alice's door.

My heartbeat picked up. Alice had never shown violent tendencies, but if things went wrong, this would probably be where it happened.

Hardy knocked for at least two minutes before a disheveled and angry Alice opened the door. By then, three other squad cars were parked on the side of the road.

Her attention flicked away from Hardy over to the cars. Alice's eyes widened. She took a step back, her hands waving in denial. The other officers were already out of their vehicles and heading up the steps.

My view was blocked by the dark blue of their police uniforms, but less than a minute later, one of them was leading a screaming, red-faced Alice down the steps. Her gaze fell onto me, and rage overtook her.

"You! I knew it was you!" She ranted and raved and called me every name under the sun until the officer forced her to lower her head and placed her inside the cruiser. The sound cut off the second the door slammed behind her.

Poppy let out an odd meow and hopped out of her hammock.

"You okay?"

She meowed again.

"I didn't bring the harness. You can't go running around out there."

The cat hopped onto my lap and pressed her paws against the window. A loud yowling noise came from her throat.

"Wait until some of them come out, and then I'll let you out, okay?"

She sat down and looked at me as if she grudgingly agreed.

I swear. Sometimes, this cat felt almost supernatural.

It took a while for some of the officers to come out. Two held a laundry basket filled with items. Poppy tracked them, watching them all the way until they got to their vehicle. A larger police van pulled up, blocking the driveway. By then, the police presence had attracted attention.

Dozens of citizens milled around, some slowing down

their vehicles so much that a traffic jam started. Hardy walked out of the house, spotted the commotion, and marched to the road, shouting and waving his arms. Most of the people standing around found better things to do, and the traffic picked up a little, but it didn't stop people from gawking.

A familiar vehicle pulled up, revealing Cole and Fletcher.

I smiled at Hardy's annoyed expression when he spotted our favorite reporter, and it turned into full-blown laughter when Cole pulled out his small notebook and Hardy started yelling at him.

Cole took a couple of steps back and held up his hands.

Fletcher wisely stayed by the car and let Cole take the brunt of Hardy's annoyance.

When two more officers left the house, Poppy let out that awful wail again, so I opened the door. "If you get lost, don't blame me, cat."

She swished her tail once and darted into Alice's house. I unfolded myself from the car and stretched, waving at Hardy when he spotted me.

His expression brightened, and he held up a finger. Jogging away from Cole, he hurried over to me. "Hey."

"Poppy ran inside the house. You might want to see what she's up to. She has a knack for this sort of thing."

Hardy pinched the space between his brows. "A crime-solving cat. The guys are going to laugh me off the force." He sounded more bemused than annoyed and went back into the house, following my errant cat.

I stayed outside and waited, not wanting to disrupt his scene. The morning air was colder than usual. Fall was officially here, the air brisk and frigid.

I didn't have long to wait. Hardy's shout sent the officers barreling back into the house with guns drawn. Apprehension trickled down my spine, but when I heard no gunfire or commotion, I settled down.

Poppy must have found something. I smiled to myself and got back into the car, leaving the door open so I could hear what was going on.

Cole came over shortly after and crouched beside the open door. His green eyes held a touch of amusement. "You ruin one story and give me another one. I'm not sure if you're a friend or the bane of my existence."

I shrugged. "I'm not sure either. This one might not be as sensational as Daniel Jensen being a cheater, but Alice's name will draw some serious attention."

"How much did she ask for?" Cole said, his expression eager.

I thought about it and decided it would come out anyway. "Three mil."

Cole's brows flew up. "Million?"

"Yes. She went for the moon."

"And landed in the ditch," Cole murmured.

Hardy came jogging out, holding Poppy in his arms like a baby. My cat looked extremely satisfied with herself. I laughed at the sight.

Cole stood up when he spotted Hardy and took a step away. Hardy set the cat in my lap.

"You wouldn't believe this if I told you," he said quietly.

I stroked Poppy's silky fur. "You'd be surprised."

Cole was giving us all an odd look, but I dismissed it.

Hardy stroked a hand over his jaw. "She found a hidden room."

I blinked down at the cat. Poppy rolled onto her back and stared at me. "Of course you did."

Cole was still staring at us.

"Everything okay?" I asked.

"You," Cole muttered. "You're my next story."

"Excuse me?"

Hardy chuckled. "I'm surprised it took you this long to realize it."

I frowned. "What are you two talking about?"

"You and your crime-solving cat." Cole shook his head in wonder. "People would love it."

The thought of being profiled in a newspaper didn't delight me as much as it seemed to delight Cole. "I don't know about that. My privacy is important to me. I don't want nosy people sniffing around my shop and home or trying to steal my cat."

"It would be a small article online for The Gazette."

"Still. Those things can take on a life of their own. What if it goes viral?"

Cole's eyes glittered. "That wouldn't be so bad, would it?"

"That's my entire point," I said. "Yes, it would be bad!"

Hardy shifted. "I'll let you two keep arguing over this. I

need to get back inside. We have another team of officers picking Jane up. They should be on the way now."

Hardy walked back into the house, leaving Cole staring at me expectantly.

"No."

"You can't just say no, Dakota!"

"I think that's what I just did," I said.

"After all I've done for you!"

I took a cleansing breath. "What about all I've done for you?"

His jaw tightened, and he looked away. Cole and I were about even on the favor front. I'd given him stories and took them away, and he'd given me tips and advice on some things that helped me to solve cases.

"I enjoy my privacy too much to blow it up with an article. The more time I spend in a job like this, the more wary I am of people. This case involved a simple but brilliant operation and almost ruined someone's career."

"Plug cameras," Cole agreed, shaking his head. "Inside the head of a screw. I think I've seen it all."

I'm glad he dropped the idea of a story, though I suspected this was a temporary reprieve. When Cole got wind of an idea, he was like a dog with a bone sometimes.

"Can you imagine?" I shuddered. "I'm going to ask Hardy to sweep my entire house when he's finished with this case."

"You know you'll have to testify, right?"

The abrupt change in subject surprised me. "Testify? Why?"

Cole laughed. "You're a brand-new P.I. and the one who pieced everything together. Daniel never reported it to the police until you handed them all the evidence on a fancy silver platter. You're going to be a major witness."

"Ugh," I said with feeling.

"Make sure all your paperwork is squared away."

I pulled my cell out and checked my email. Things had been so busy I'd forgotten about the rest of the things I was waiting on for my license.

To my delight, I had everything I needed to finalize things.

"I'll have everything ready, but I wasn't technically a P.I. when I solved this case."

"Nonetheless, don't be surprised if it happens."

"Nothing surprises me anymore," I muttered.

Cole laughed and tapped the roof of the car. "Take care of yourself. This isn't the end of the crime-solving kitty."

"Cole!"

He laughed and walked away.

TWENTY-NINE

Later that evening, Cole forwarded an email with the link to the front page of The Gazette. A bold, all-caps headline screamed *Heiress of Major Newspaper Conglomerate Arrested on Multiple Felony Charges.*

I grimaced but clicked the article anyway and skimmed through. Jane was barely a blip in the article. Cole had focused most of it on Alice, though Alice wouldn't have been able to do any of this without the help of someone skilled in IT.

It figured that the socialite, even when committing a major felony, would gain the most notoriety. It didn't matter, though. Jane would receive a similar sentence to Alice, so both would be in prison for quite a while.

Hopefully.

Poppy lay curled beside me on the sofa, purring contentedly as I scratched behind her ears. I'd given her a few extra treats for helping Hardy uncover the hidden room, which revealed multiple computers and surveillance. Whatever Jane was doing, she was doing it to multiple people.

Whether Jane was a reader or an aspiring author or neither had yet to be determined—not that it mattered anymore. Maybe she was so adamant about receiving an advanced copy to throw me off her trail. Or maybe she really was a huge fan.

Hardy had to get home to his daughter this evening, though I'd come home to a large bouquet of stunning flowers and a sweet card thanking me for many things, mostly for choosing my safety over solving the case.

It had taken this long for me to realize I could do both.

The doorbell rang, signaling my food delivery. I was too tired to cook or do much of anything after Hardy dropped me off a few hours ago.

But to my surprise, opening the door revealed not only my food but Daniel Jensen.

"Hi," I said.

He handed the brown paper bag to me. "Can I come in?"

I stepped back and motioned him in. "Of course. Though I'm afraid I only have enough food for one tonight."

"Don't worry about it. I dropped by without calling."

I shut the door behind us and headed into the kitchen. "I have enough wine if you'd like a glass."

Daniel smiled. "I'll take you up on that one."

I poured us both a glass and took my takeout into the living room.

While I ate, Daniel talked.

"You saved me."

I stopped eating and stared at him. "You're my friend. What else would I have done?"

His fingers curled around his glass as he watched me eat. Normally, I'd feel uncomfortable, but it was Daniel, and we'd eaten together a million times.

"I can think of a hundred times and a hundred instances where I was in trouble, and a friend never went as far as you did to make sure I was okay."

"Then maybe they weren't a very good friend."

"I don't think that's it," Daniel said. "I think you're such a good friend that the thought of letting anyone down is unfathomable to you."

I blushed. "Someone was blackmailing you. I couldn't let them get away with it."

"You saved my career, Dakota. That's not a small thing." He exhaled and pulled something out of his pocket. "This is an invitation to my publisher. They want you to come visit them."

I took it, shock rooting me to my seat. "Why?"

"I'd like to think it's because they're very good people and they want to reward noble and heroic people." He took a sip of wine. "But I'm also levelheaded enough to know you saved one of their major money makers and they're thankful for it. Plus, you managed to help me dodge a major scandal."

I shrugged. "All in a day's work."

Daniel shook his head. "No. It was you and your hard work and critical thinking skills. Don't try to undermine yourself. Not around me."

"There's nothing I can say except you're welcome, and you will receive my bill very soon."

He clinked his glass against mine. "And I shall happily pay it."

We sat in silence for a while, the only sound the occasional scrape of the fork against my plate.

When he spoke again, his tone was a little more somber. "You're happy?"

I waited a little while to respond, taking the time to thoroughly examine where I was and what I wanted in my life and how it related to him. "I am."

"He is what you want?"

I set my fork down. "He was always what I wanted. We just had some bumps in the road."

"I see." Daniel exhaled and shook his head. "I hope we can always be friends. You are important to me, and I want you in my life."

"Of course we can. Hardy says I have to have a chess chaperone now, but he's fine with us hanging out." I shrugged. "I think he wants to catch you cheating just as badly as I do."

Daniel laughed and stood, taking his wine glass with him. "I don't know how many times I have to tell you I'm not cheating. Maybe one day you both will understand I am simply that good."

He walked to the kitchen and washed his glass out, setting it carefully on the towel next to the sink.

"You're definitely cheating!" I called. "Your reign of chess terror won't last much longer!"

"Says you!" Daniel said on the way out. "Next week. Same time, same place?"

"You betcha!"

His chuckle followed him out, and when silence fell over my living room again, I smiled and turned the television on, content with my simple life and the few friends I had.

EPILOGUE
SIX MONTHS LATER

The diamond sparkled under the gymnasium light, making me catch my breath the same way it had for the last two weeks.

Engaged.

I was *engaged*.

The proposal wasn't epic or planned to death, and it happened just the way I wanted. I wasn't the kind of person who wanted attention or some grandiose public proposal.

All I ever wanted was Hardy.

It happened one morning over pancakes and coffee, one of the few weekends we could have a sleepover together. Izzy was staying with a family member, and Hardy had woken me up with breakfast in bed.

I'd never forget it.

He'd set the tray over me, dropped a quick kiss on my lips, and crawled back into bed next to me.

I'd just cut into my pancakes when he spoke.

"Dakota?"

"Hmm?" Hardy made amazing pancakes. Real maple syrup, real salted butter. Yum.

"I love you, you know that?"

I'd laughed because, of course, I knew that.

"And you know Izzy loves you, too?"

Tears sprang to my eyes over that one. I'd loved that little girl the moment I'd spoken to her in the ice cream parlor. It just took me a while to figure out.

I nodded and put my fork down, catching Hardy's eyes as he spoke.

"We've been together a while now, minus that unfortunate break. Every moment I'm awake, I always wish I was spending it with you."

My breath caught. There was no way he was doing this...was he?

"We don't have to get married now. Or even soon. We can wait a year or two. Whatever. I don't care. I want to make a promise to you...that this is it for me. You're my person, Dakota. You're the only one I want. I know things are complicated. I know you're adjusting to being my girl-friend and a role model to Izzy, but we both love you." He exhaled and closed his eyes. "I'm asking you to be my wife."

I didn't say anything at first, carefully sliding the tray away and standing to pick it up and set it on the floor. Then I launched myself at Hardy, his rumbling laughter echoing against my ear as he caught me against his chest.

"Yes," I whispered. "Of course I'll be your wife."

Which brought us to today, watching Izzy graduate from kindergarten. The paperwork was signed, severing her mother's rights, and Hardy was her sole guardian. It had broken both our hearts, but I'd sworn to always be there for her. If her mother couldn't or wouldn't, no matter what happened between me and Hardy, I would always be available to her. She was just that special.

The principal called her name. Hardy and I launched to our feet, screaming and yelling her name. Izzy's blush was evident all the way to the bleachers, but a small smile curved over her lips as she accepted the fake diploma the principal handed to her.

They stopped to take a picture, and Hardy and I waved like crazy people.

And just like that, it was over.

Izzy was officially a first grader.

I was engaged.

And things had never been better.

ALSO BY S.E. BABIN

A Shelf Indulgence Cozy Mystery Series

How about a ghost whisperer in a new magical town? Check out
The Psychic Cleaner series!

Psychic Cleaner

Like a little more magic with your cozies? Check out The
Magical Soapmaker Mysteries!

The Magical Soapmaker Mysteries

If you'd like a little more action and sass and don't mind some
PG-13 language, check out my Aphrodite series.

The Goddess Chronicles

Or, if you like a snarky bartender with a secretive mixed heritage,
meet Violet!

Cocktails in Hell

ABOUT THE AUTHOR

Sheryl likes cake too much and can be found hoarding it while hiding from her children in the pantry closet.

Follow her on Amazon at: https://www.amazon.com/S-E-Babin/e/B00J1J236A

9 781648 397431